TRANSPORT

ACTIVITY
BOOK

1 Transport is a means by which people and goods are taken or carried from one place to another. Pick out transport means and circle them.

Car	Truck	Book

Helicopter	Bus	Train

Ship	playing cards	Pen

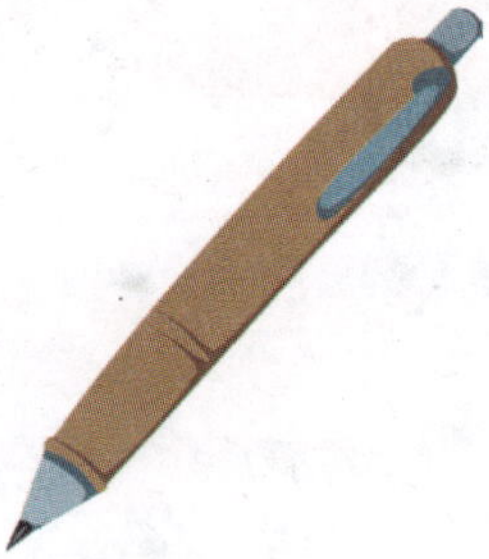

2

2 Transport can be public or private. Private transport is owned by an individual while the Public transport is for all the people. Identify Public and Private vehicles given below.

3 Complete the words by looking at the pictures.

A_RPLA_E YA__HT SH__P

TR__IN H__LICO__TER S__BMA__INE

 Draw a line from the picture to its name.

Hot air balloon

Ship

Bus

Train

Truck

Taxi

Transportation can be done by various means like land, air, water, space, rail and cable. Match the transports below with its mode.

Air

Rail

Space

Land

Water

Land transport is transportation through road. Circle the pictures depicting road transport.

Land transport can be of many types. They can be two-wheeler, four-wheeler or many-wheeler. Colour the pictures which are the means of land transport.

8 Pick out and colour four-wheeled land vehicles.

9 See the below pictures and circle the many-wheeled land vehicles.

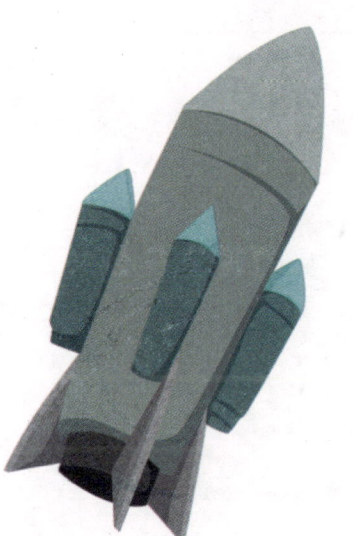

10 Label the transports below. Use the names from the clue box.

Train | Taxi | Ambulance | Cycle | Truck | Bus

 Draw a line from the picture to its correct description.

Four-wheeler

One-wheeler

Many-wheeler

Six-wheeler

Transport used to carry goods is called goods transport. It can be transported by any means. Trace the names of goods transport shown below.

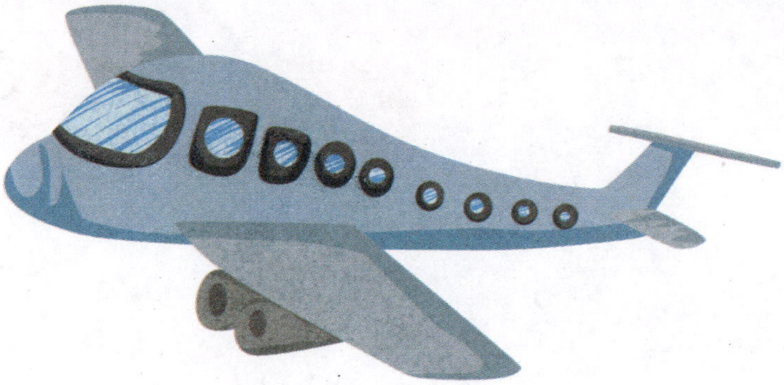

Aeroplane

Ship

Train

Truck

Learn to draw a truck in four easy steps. Follow the below instructions to make one.

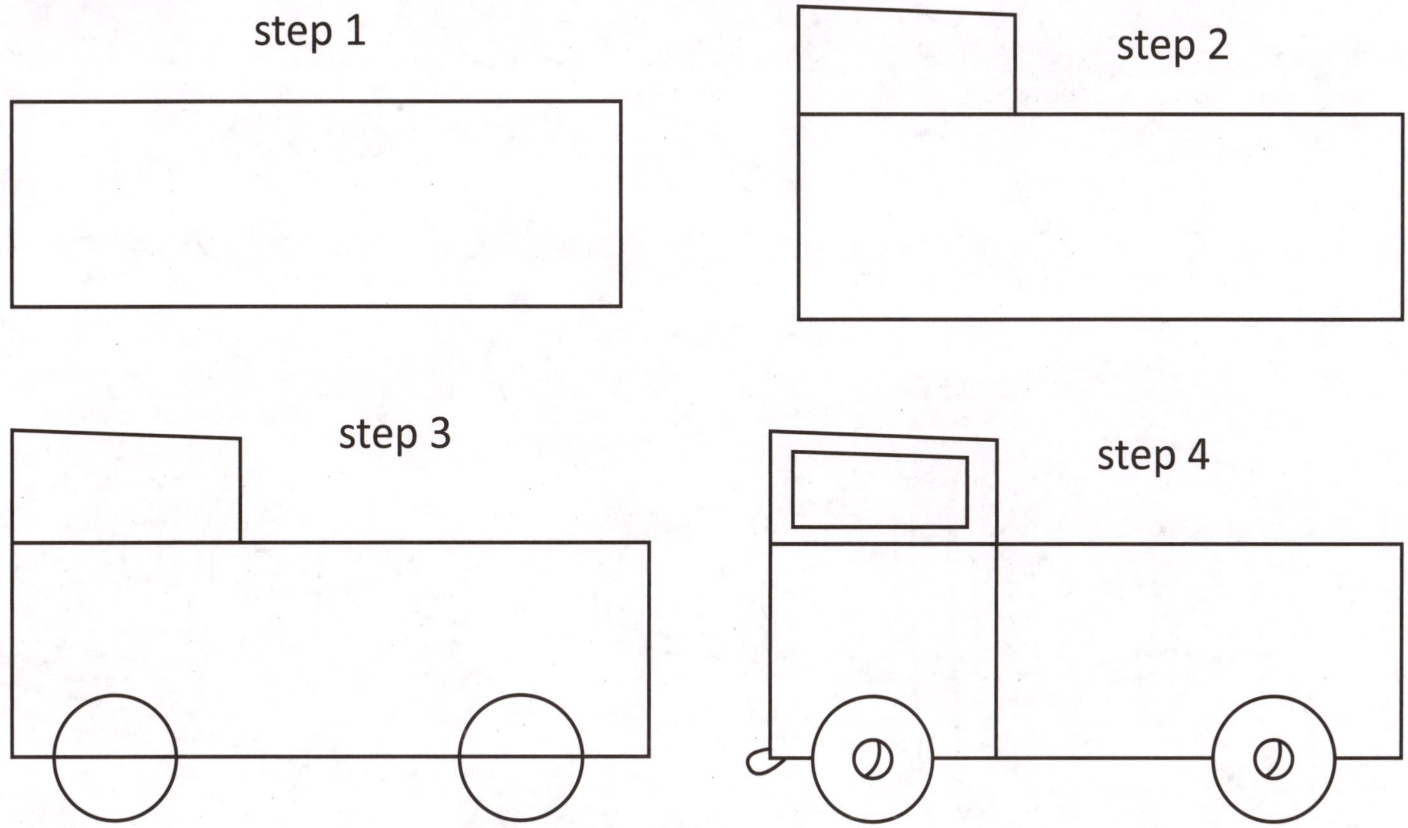

step 1

step 2

step 3

step 4

14 Colour and name the vehicle below.

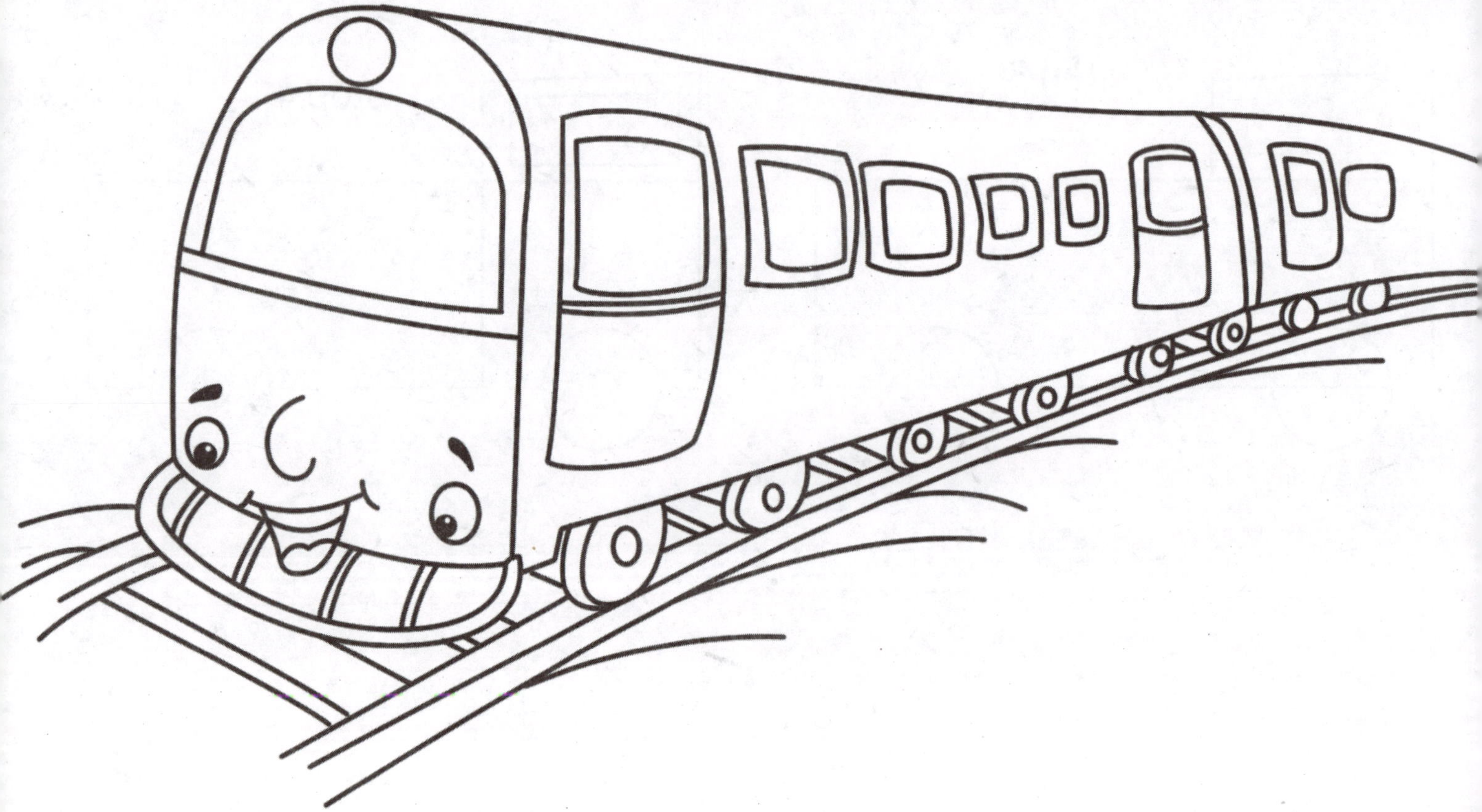

15 Cut and paste pictures of the means of road transport from the transport chart.

16 Transportation through air is called Air transport. Stick a smiley against the below means of air transport.

 Parachute making is easy and quick. Follow the below indicated steps to make one.

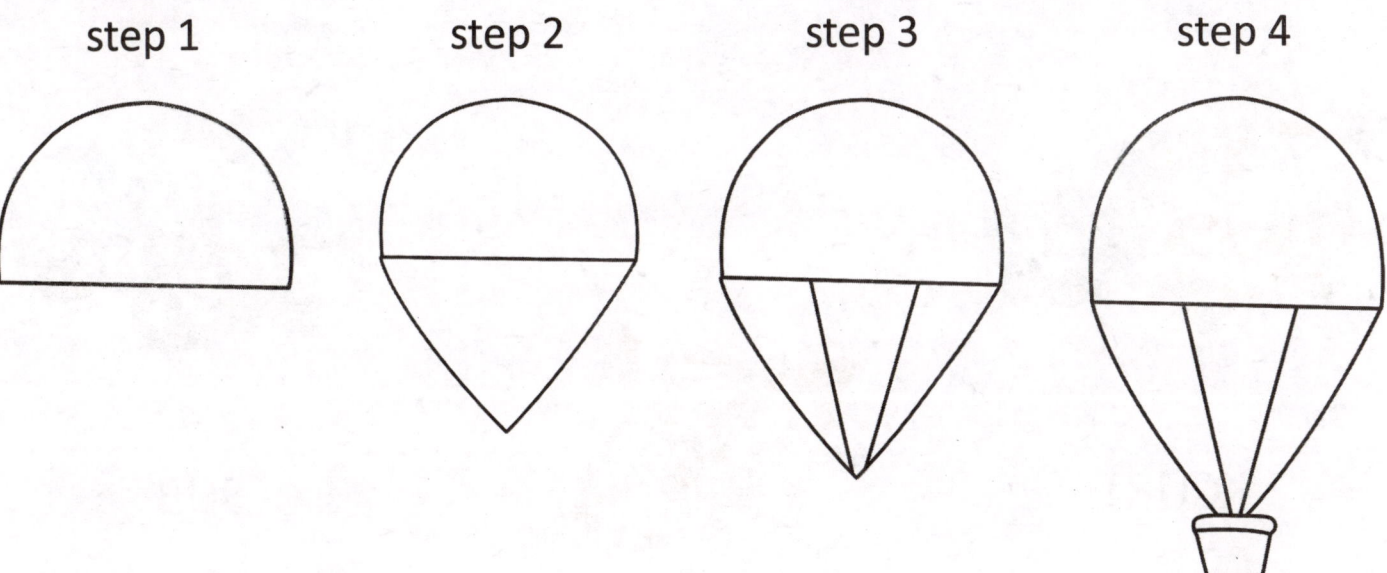

step 1   step 2   step 3   step 4

18 Unscramble the letters to make the correct word with the help of pictures.

KCURT

_____

PIHS

_____

SUB

_____

ENARC

_____

ENALPRIA

_____

ENIRAMBUS

_____

19 Given below is the picture of sky. Cut and paste all the means of air transport from the transport chart and paste them in the sky.

20 Water transport or Marine transport is transportation through sea. Identify the means of sea transport and colour them.

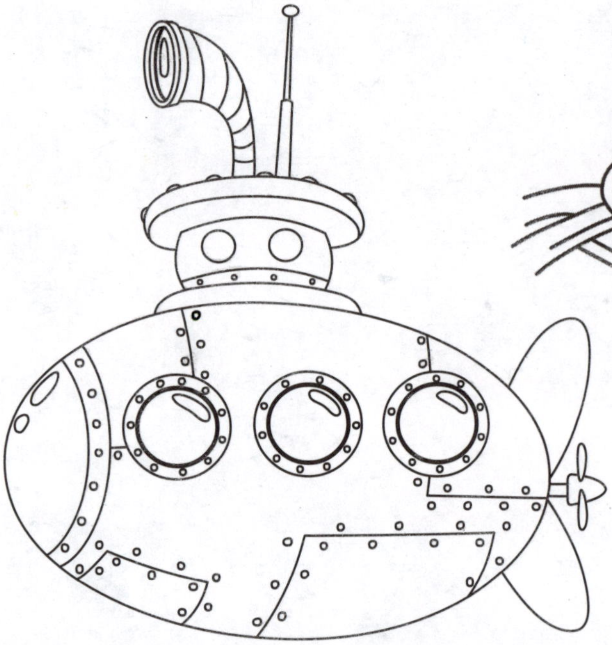

 Make a ship with the below shown easy techniques.

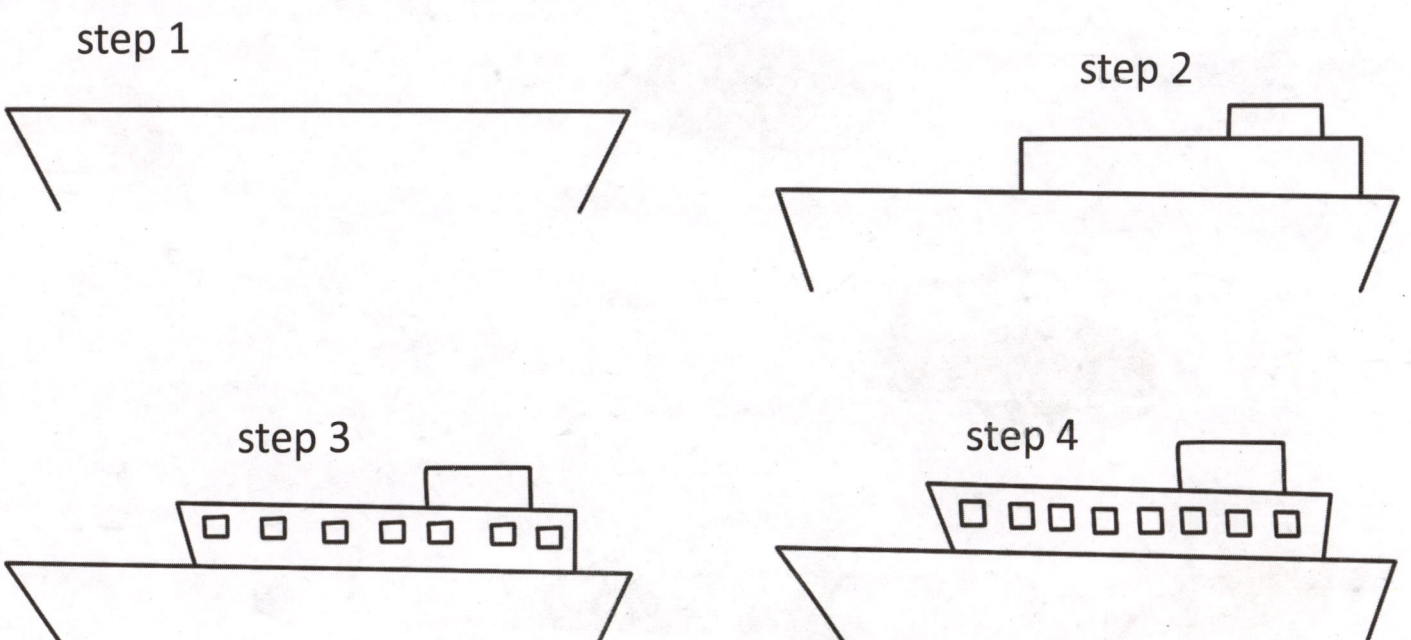

step 1

step 2

step 3

step 4

22

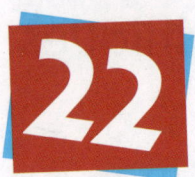

Draw a line to match the vehicles to their correct means of transport.

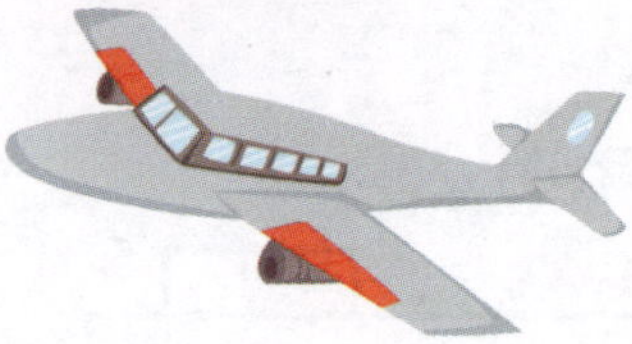

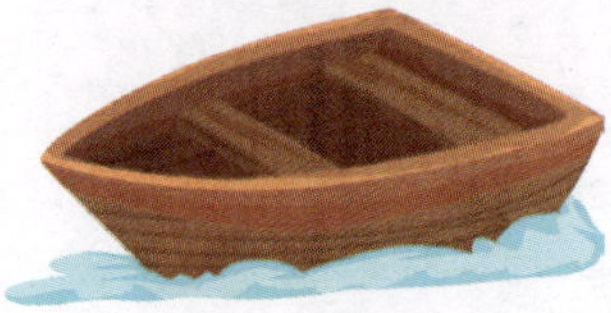

Land

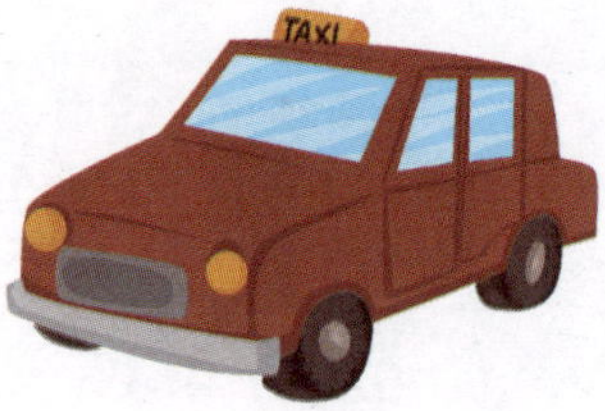

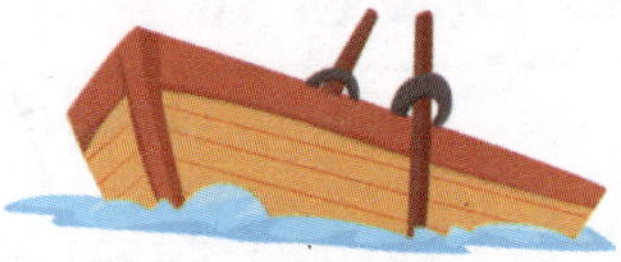

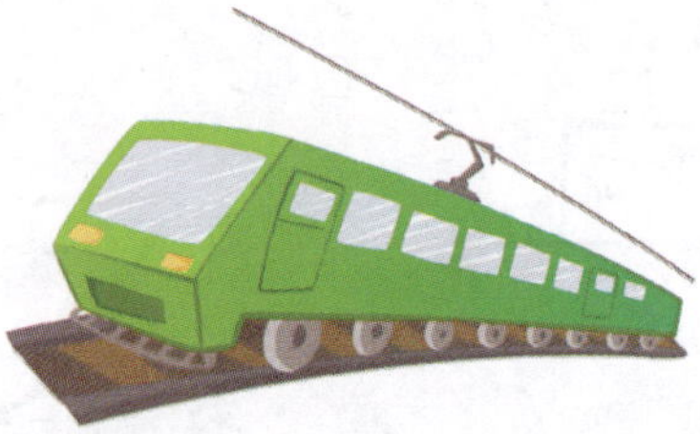

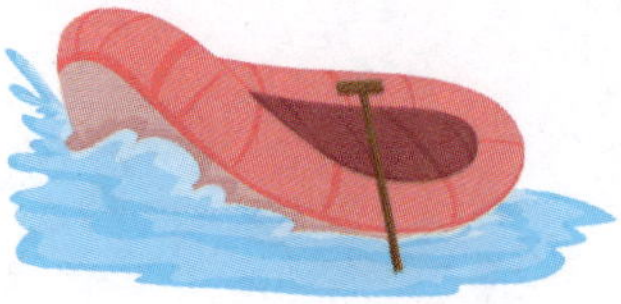

Air

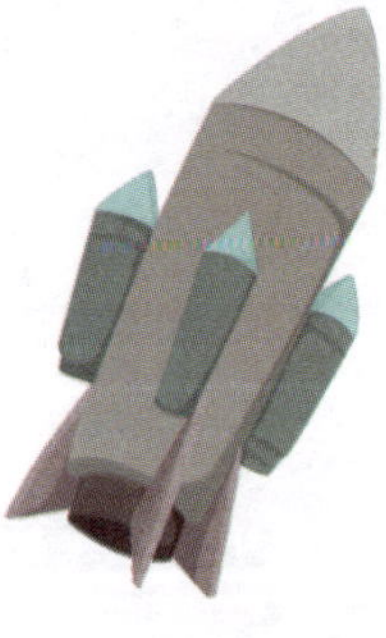

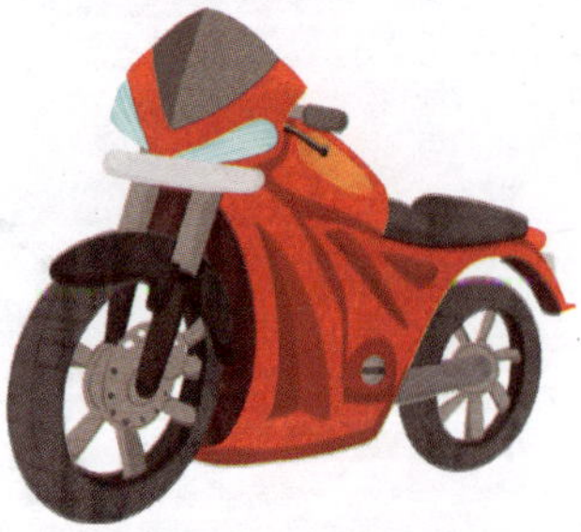

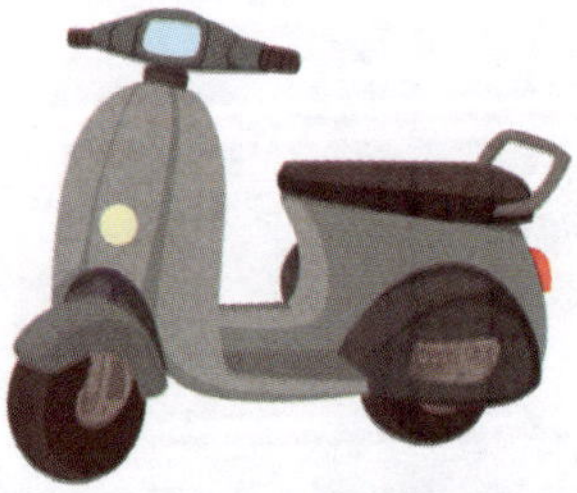

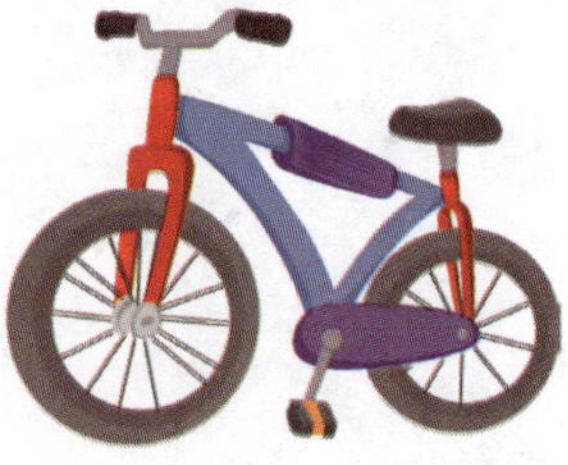

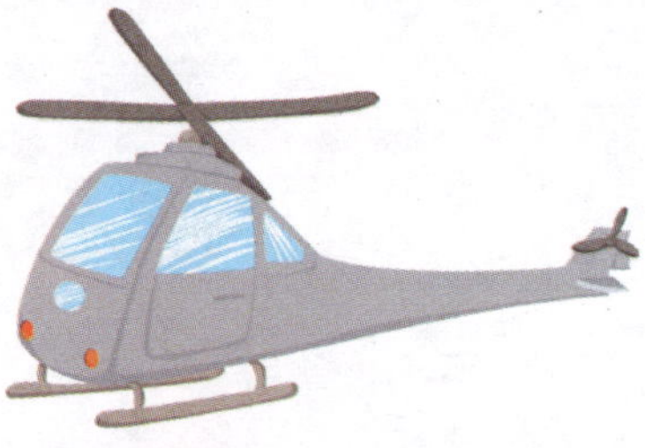

Sea

Look at the pictures below. There are three names given with each picture. Identify the picture and circle its correct name.

van, truck, car submarine, rocket, boat train, bike, bicycle

airplane, rocket, car train, tire, hot air balloon

sled, ship, submarine rocket, ambulance, skate bike, tire, wheel

 Fill in the blanks with correct words.

Airplane / **Land** / **Helicopter** / **Ship** / **Boat** / **Yacht** / **Bicycle** / **Bus**

1. _____ sails in water.

2. _____ has two wheels.

3. Car, truck, bus are the means of _____ transport.

4. People travel through ____ and ____ in sea.

5. Air transports are ____ and _____.

6. _____ carries many passengers.

 Join the dots to complete the picture. Now identify it and write its name below the picture.

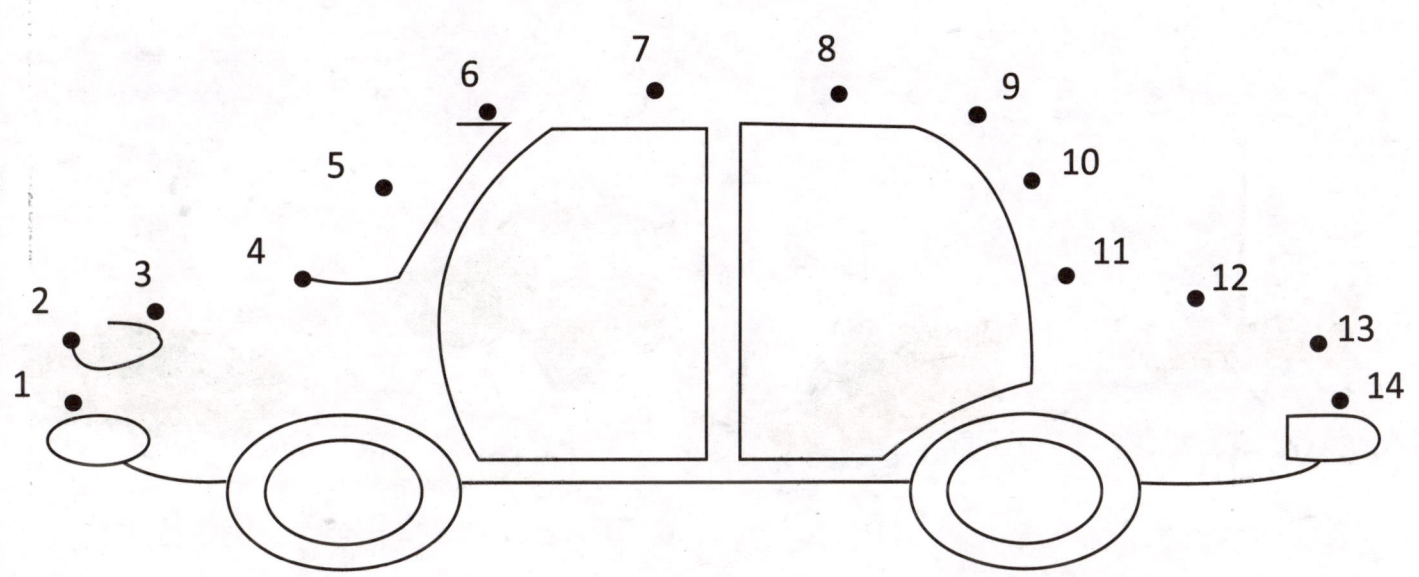

_____

26 Pick the odd one out.

Truck   Ship   Car   Bus

Yacht   Ship   Truck   Boat

Airplane   Hot air balloon   Helicopter   Ship

27

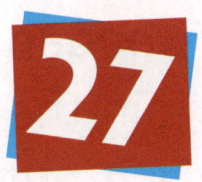

Colour the below means of air transport and name it.

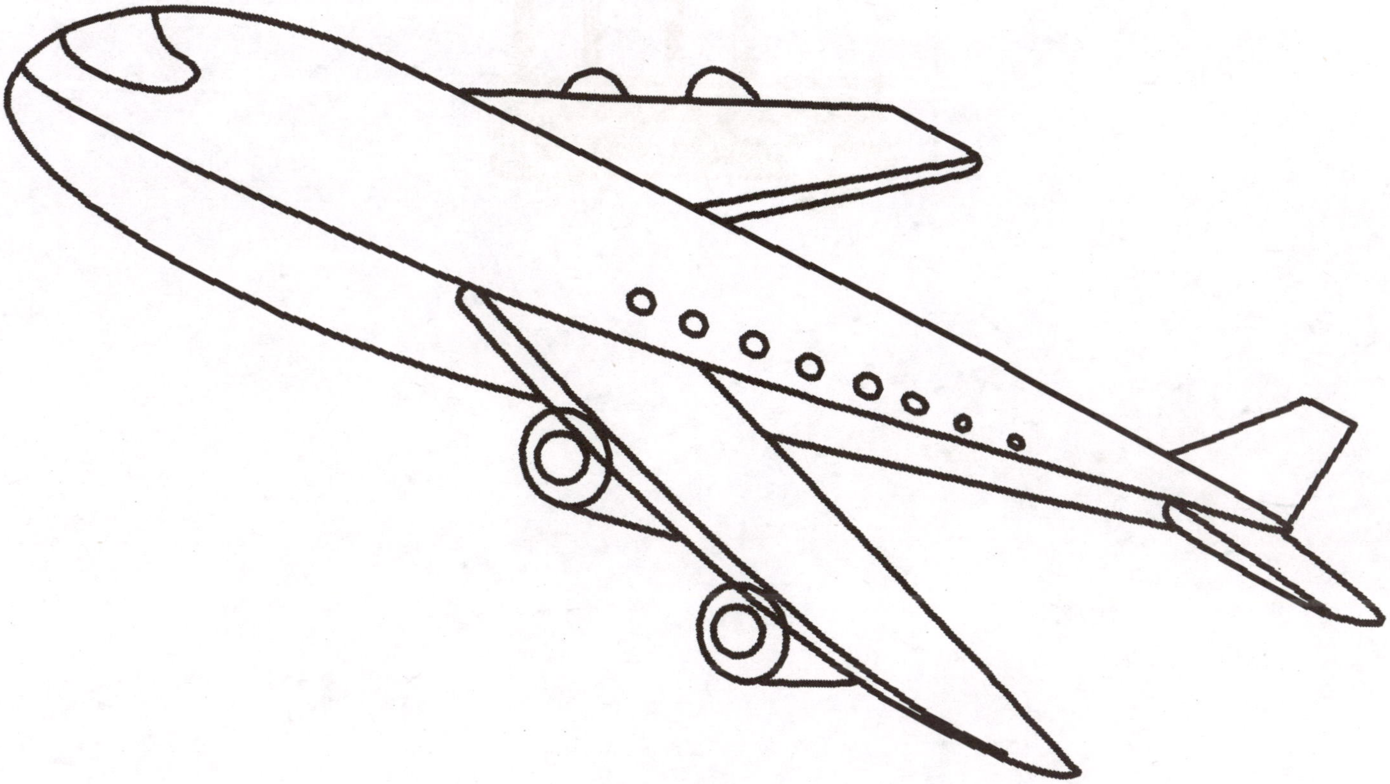

____

28 Make your own car. Take 3 big and 5 small wooden sticks. Stick the 3 big sticks with glue and join the rest 4 at their back at 90 degrees. Now place the remaining 1 small stick at the tip of the four sticks as shown in the picture. Stick 2 big black buttons at the base of your car to form tires. Your car is ready.

 Match the vehicles to the modes of transport they use.

 Paste the pictures of different means of transport below from the transport chart.

Underwater transport is the transportation means used under water. Colour the picture and understand the underwater mode of transportation.

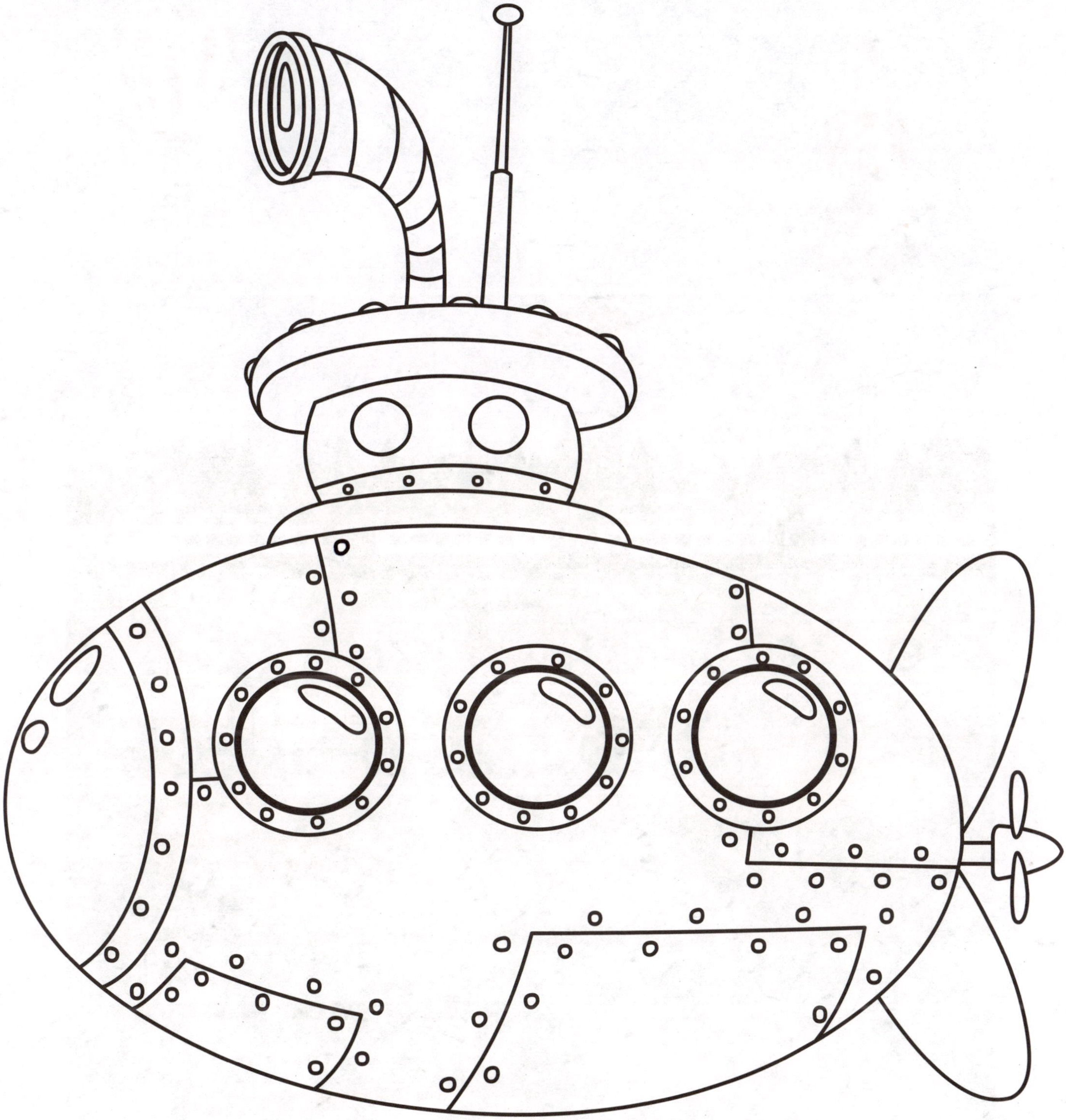

32 Can you figure out different means of transportation in this picture? Identify them.

 Fill in the columns with corresponding numbered pictures.

Across
2. jet
4. truck
6. helicopter
7. airplane

Down
1. motorcycle
3. tank
5. ship

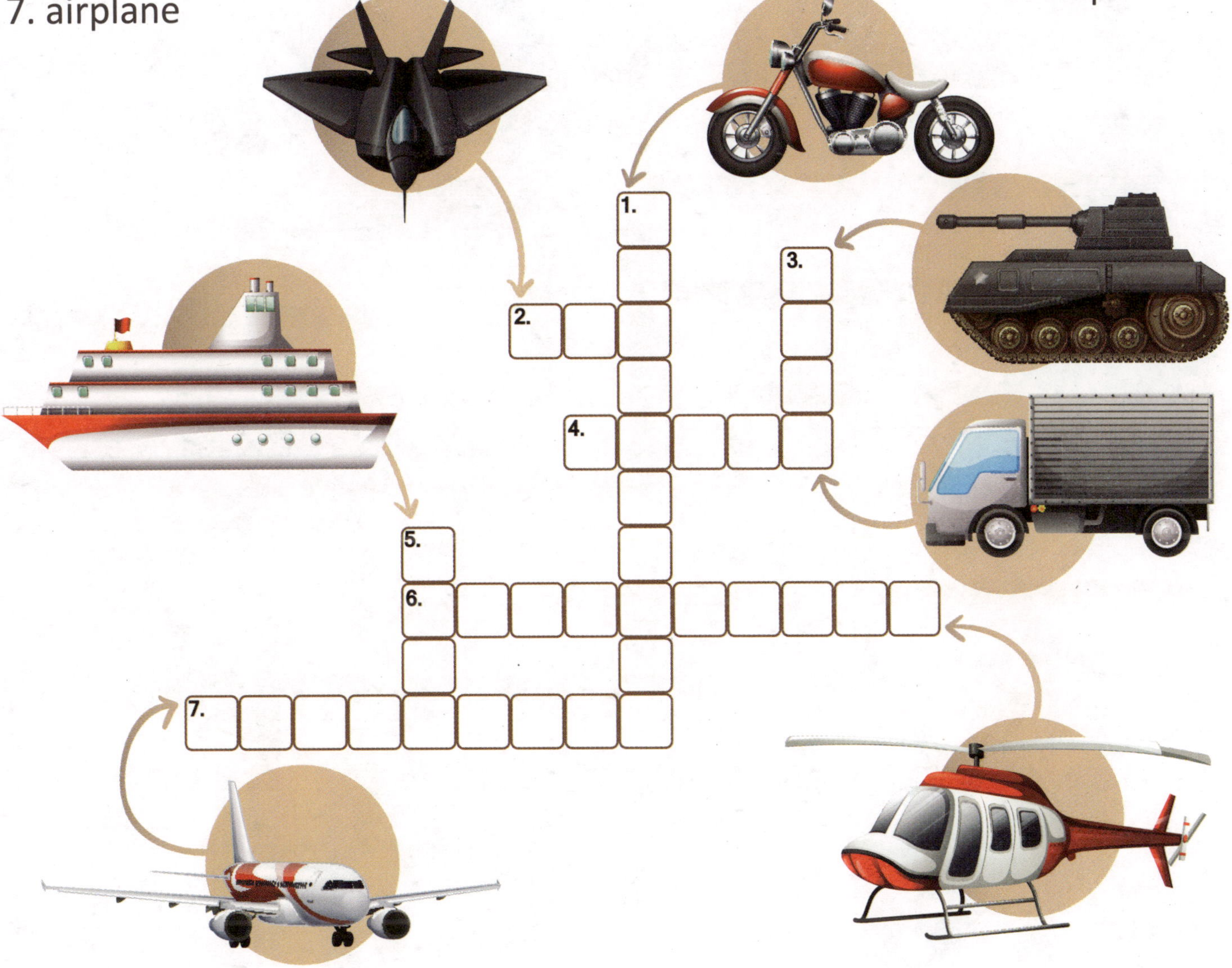

34 Help Jack reach the ship.

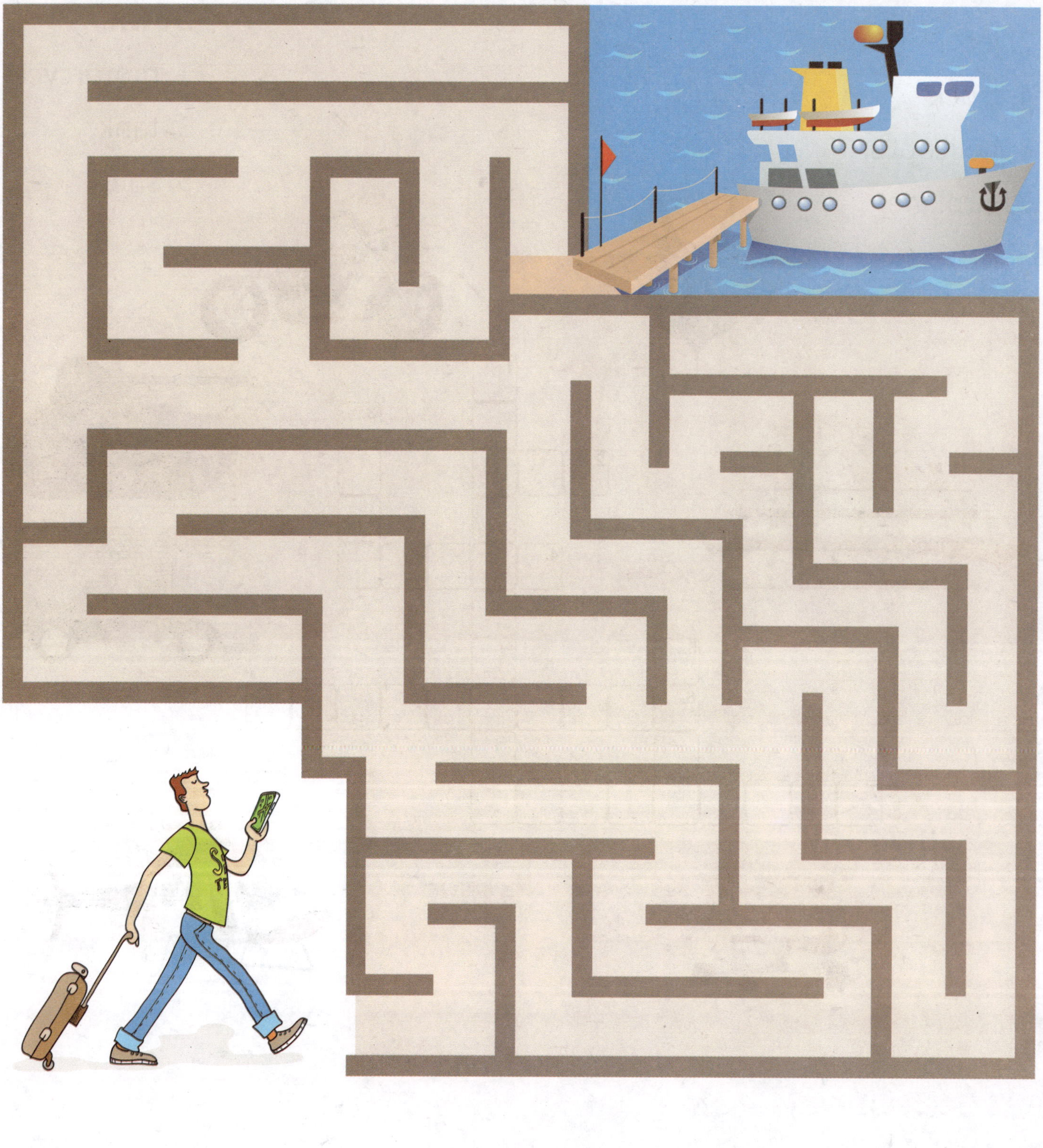

Hauling by the medium of rail is called rail transport. Pictures of different types of trains are given below. Imitate the pictures to draw and colour them.

Identify the differences in these two pictures and circle them.

Arrange the below means of transport from small to big. Number them in ascending order.

train

bus

car

_____ _____ _____

airplane _____

boat bicycle hot air balloon

_____ _____ _____

38 Colour the hot air balloon given below.

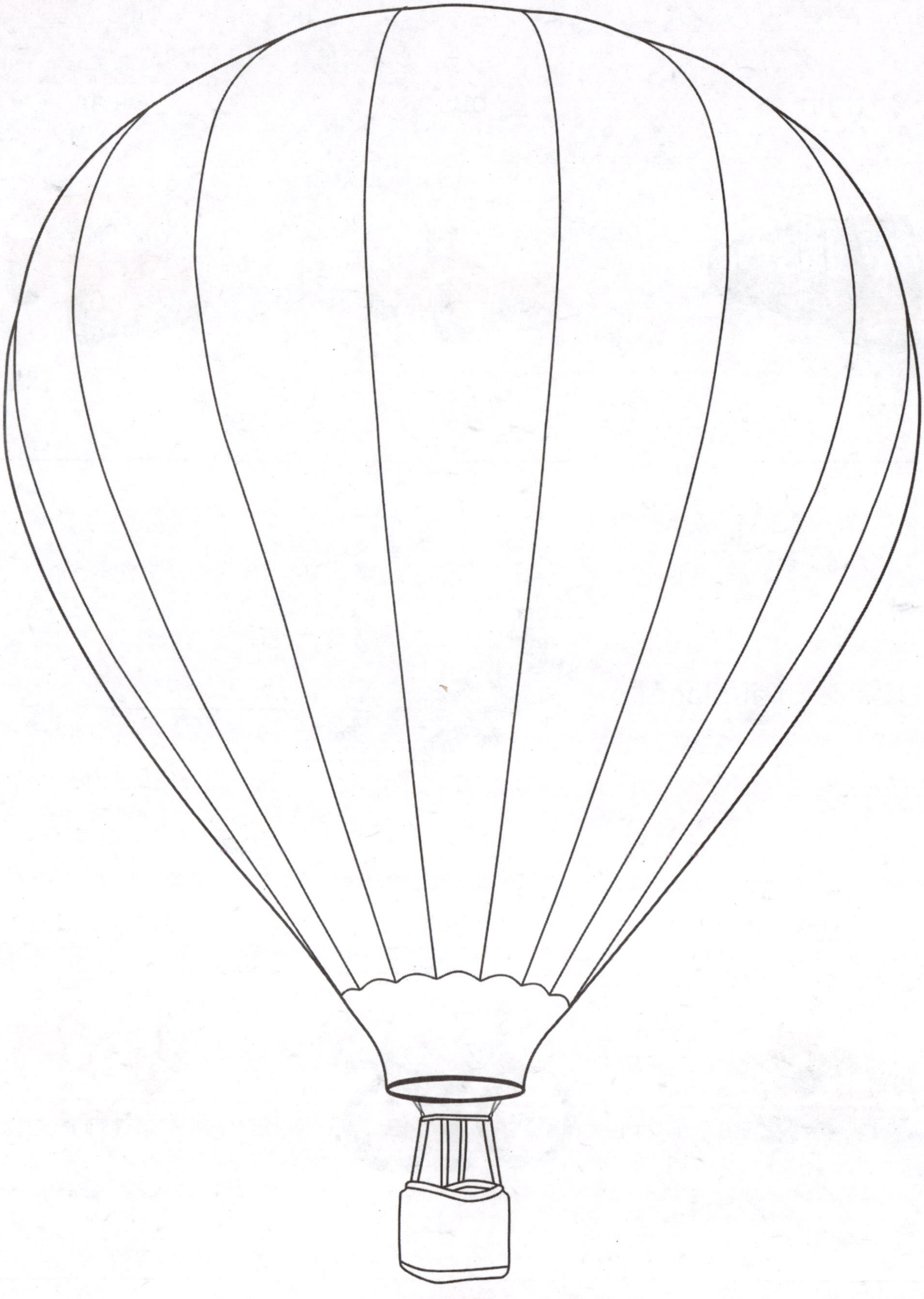

Find out the hidden means of transport given in the grid below.

E	C	A	R	Q	T	R	A	I	N	F	B
S	L	J	G	F	D	J	B	B	S	H	I
A	T	X	J	W	A	G	O	N	O	J	C
K	R	V	M	K	G	J	A	V	I	K	Y
G	U	B	S	L	S	K	T	Q	Y	L	C
H	C	N	H	A	H	L	R	P	O	I	L
L	K	B	U	A	I	R	P	L	A	N	E
C	V	I	T	W	P	F	H	L	N	M	X
N	Z	K	T	S	D	V	X	K	J	T	Z
M	H	E	L	I	C	O	P	T	E	R	X
Q	X	E	E	Y	U	I	O	P	T	A	V
S	U	B	M	A	R	I	N	E	K	M	U

Car   Wagon   Truck   Helicopter   Boat

Bicycle   Airplane   Submarine   Ship   Bike

Jet   Shuttle   Train   Tram

Want to make a truck? Here's how.

Collect 8 wooden sticks and divide them into two equal parts. Now you have 2 groups of 4 sticks. Put one group horizontal over the vertical laid group and glue them. Stick two big black button to show tyres. The truck is ready.

41 Cut and paste all the means of water transport on the water from the transport chart.

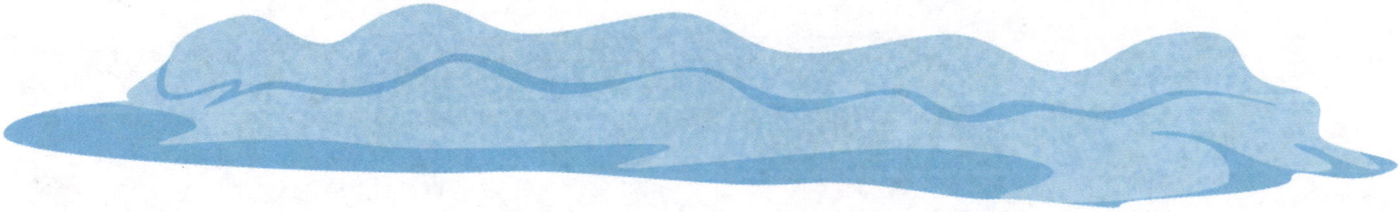

 Pick the odd one out.

   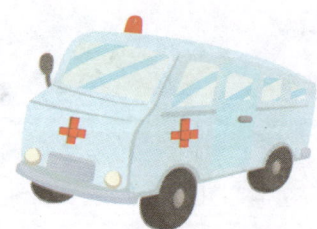

 Fill in the blanks.

Fastest means of transport _____

Slowest means of transport _____

Largest means of transport _____

Smallest means of transport _____

44 Number the following means of transport in order of their speed.

45 Identify the below modes of transport and tick the correct answer.

- ☐ Land Transport
- ☐ Water Transport
- ☐ Air Transport

- ☐ Land Transport
- ☐ Water Transport
- ☐ Air Transport

- ☐ Land Transport
- ☐ Water Transport
- ☐ Air Transport

46

Rocket making cannot be simpler than this. Just follow the below steps.

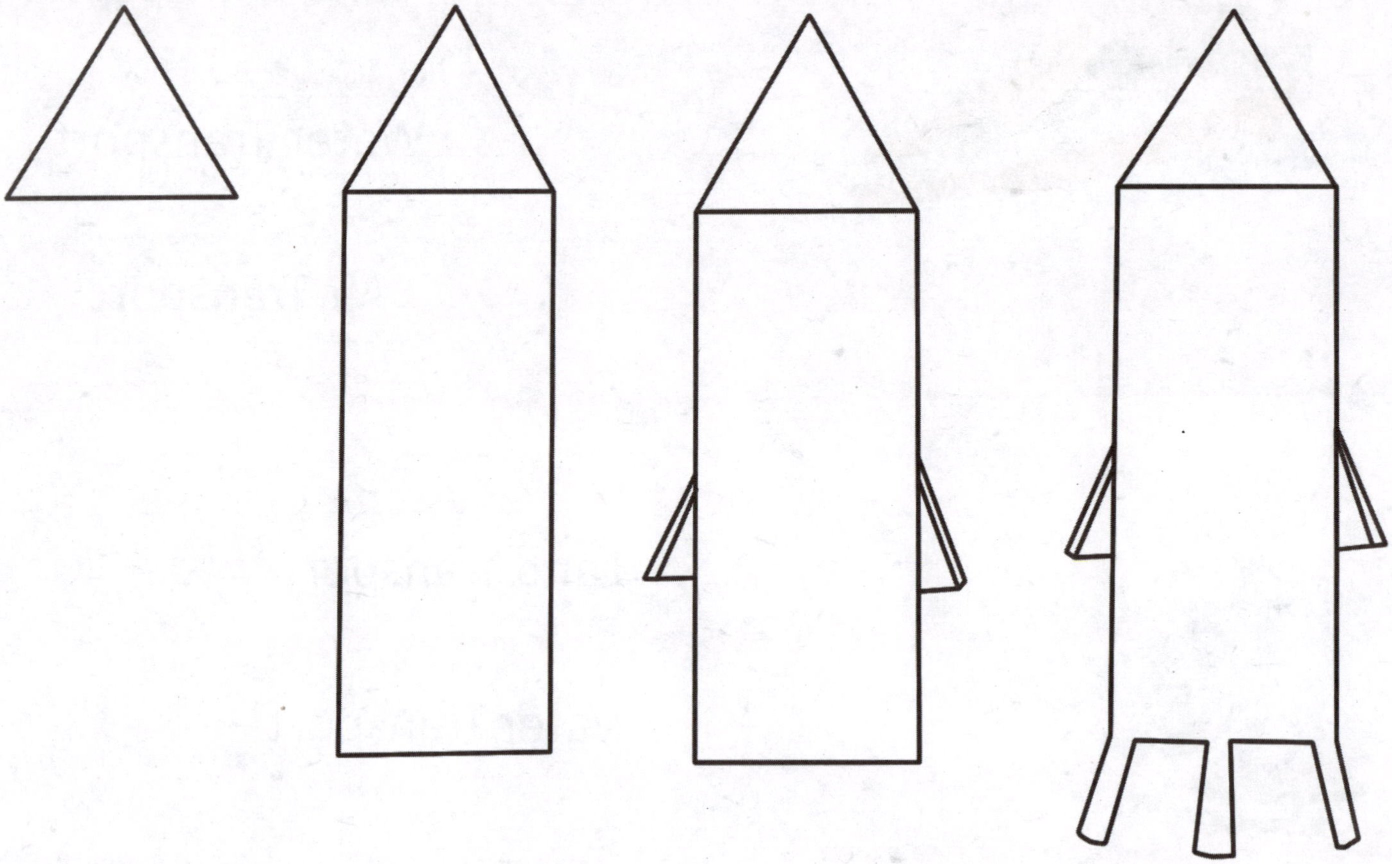

47 Paste a picture of spacecraft and space shuttle below to depict space transport.

48 Colour the below picture of ship.

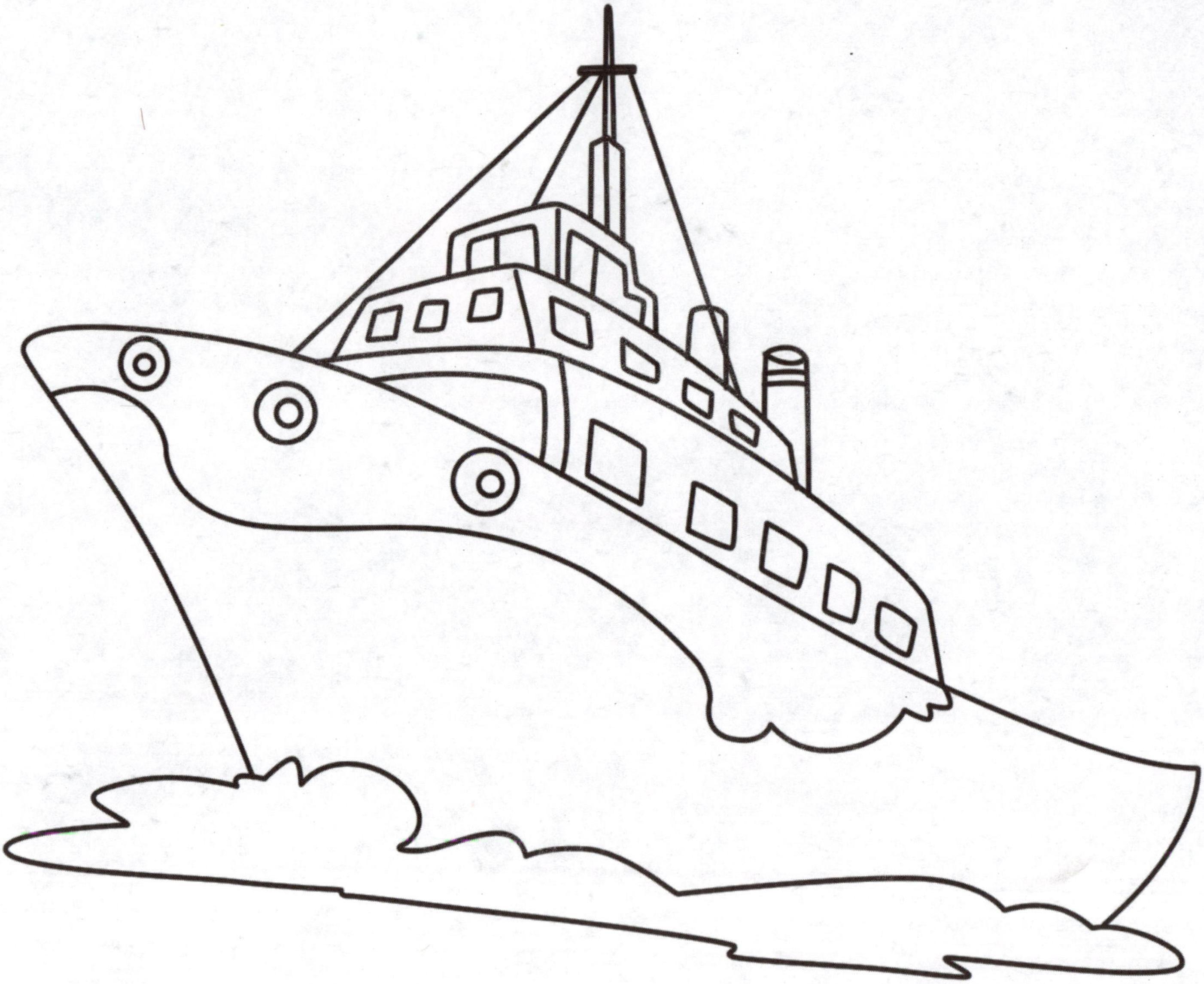

Write down the names of the following vehicles using the words given in the box below.

Airplane / Car / Train / Ship / Boat / Yacht

50 Join dot to dot to complete the picture and colour it.

50

51 Stick a star against those which are cable transport.

Match the front half of each vehicle with its back.

53 Colour the below means of transport and write down its name as well.

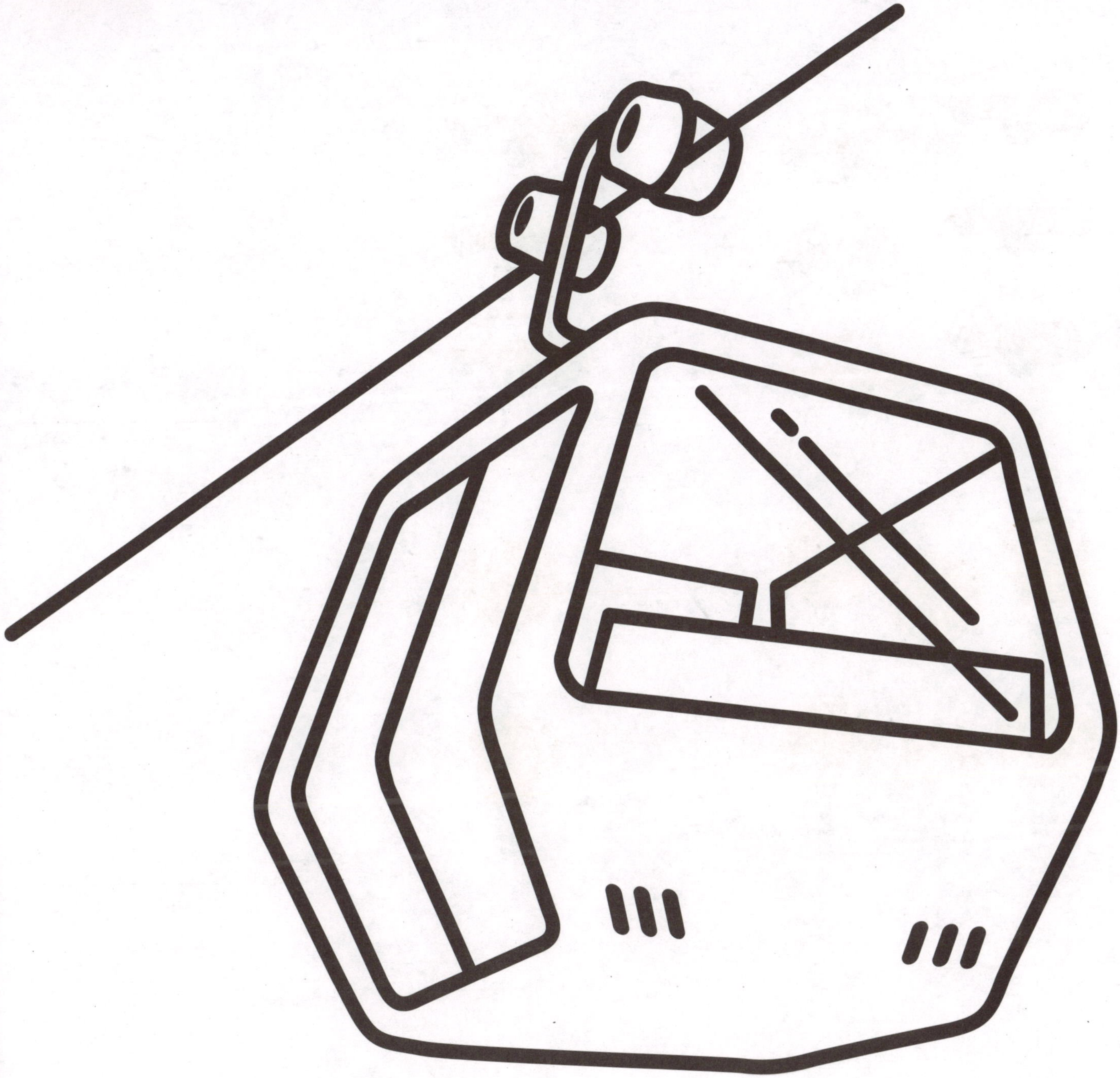

_____

54 Count the means of transport given below and do the sum.

 +  = _____

 +  = _____

 +  = _____

55 Paste any two means of cable transport in the space provided below.

The astronaut is preparing for a space trip. Help the astronaut reach his spacecraft located at some distance.

57

Look at the pictures of Jeep given below. They all appear same but they are not. Find the two similar pictures.

1

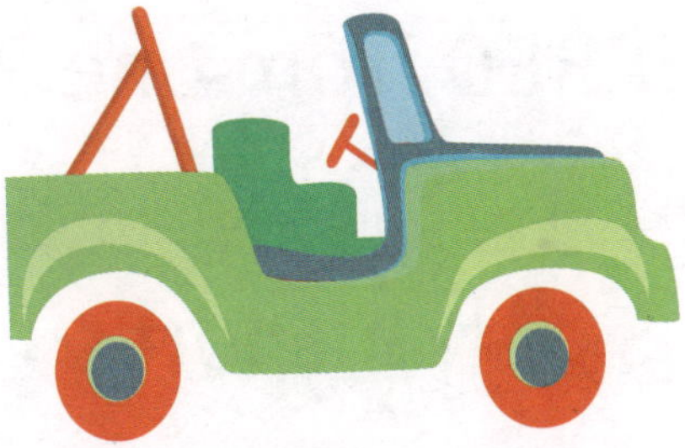

2

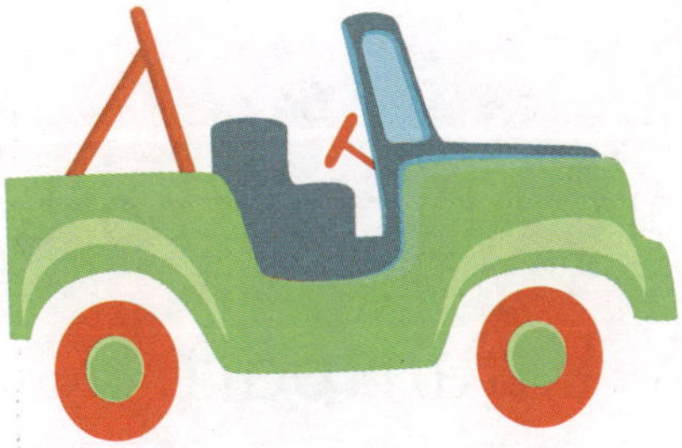

3

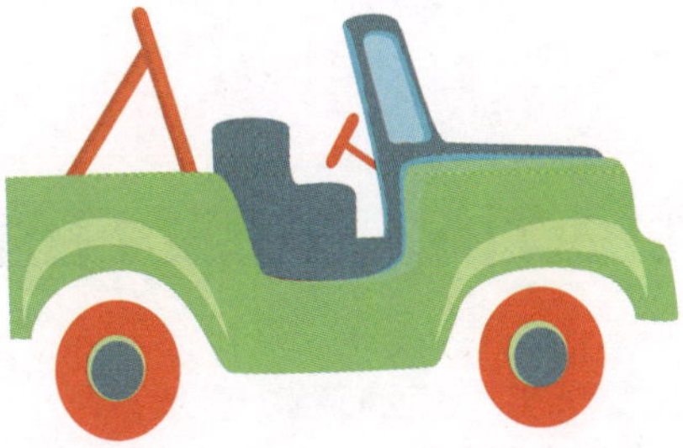

7

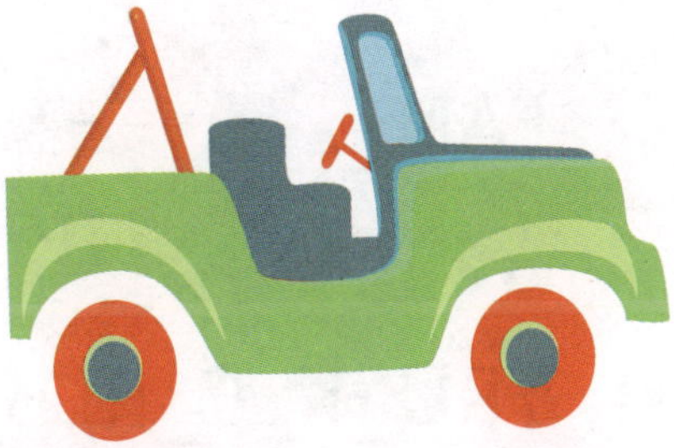

4

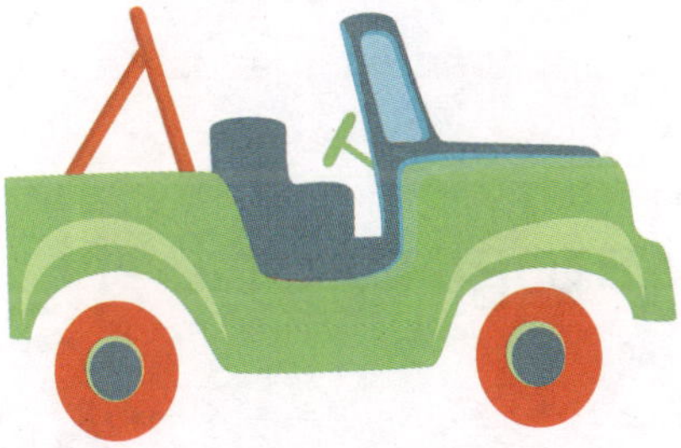

5

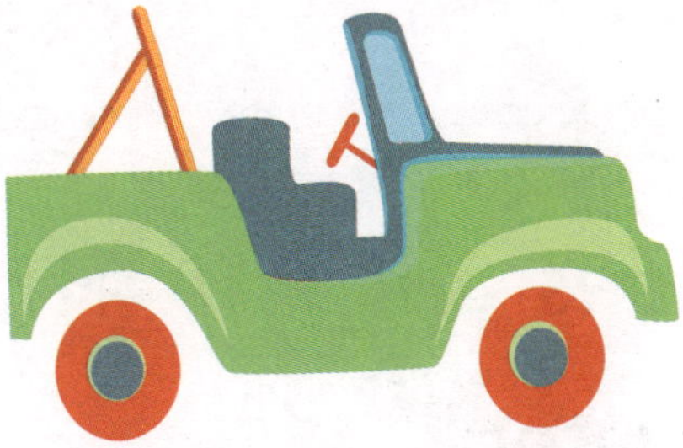

6

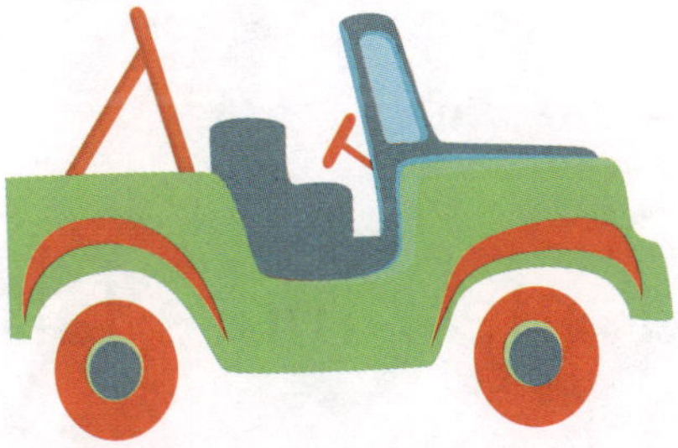

Fill in the blanks.

- TRA_SPORT is the means by which PE_PLE, animals and goods can be TRANS_ERRED from one PLA_E to another.

- There are many MOD_S of transport.

- These are LA_D transport, WAT_R transport, AI_ transport, SP_CE transport, CA_LE transport and RA_L transport.

- Land transport is transferring things and people through LAN_.

- TRU_K, C_R, B_S and more come in the category of LAN_ transport.

- Water transport includes SHI_, YA_HT, BO_T and other vehicles that float on water.

- PARAC_UTE, AIR_LANE, HELI_OPTER and a few more fall under air transport category.

59 Rearrange the jumbled words.

KCURT   _____

RAC _____

RTEOCK _____

PCHAARETU _____

OTAB _____

CHLTRAIFI _____

LABCE _____

60

How do we go to school? Circle the correct options.

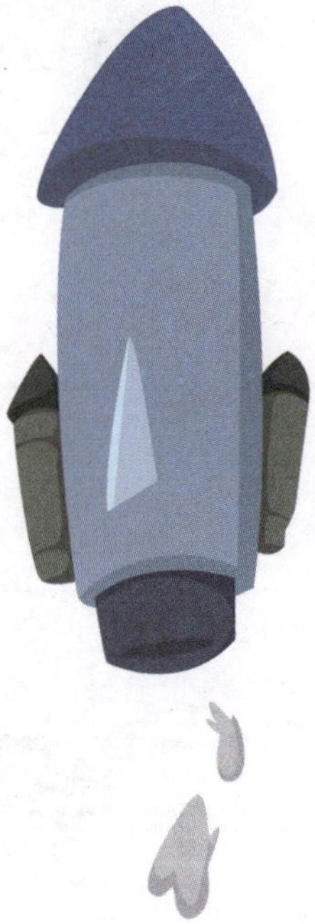

 Tank making is easy and fun. Try making tank with the help of the below demonstration.

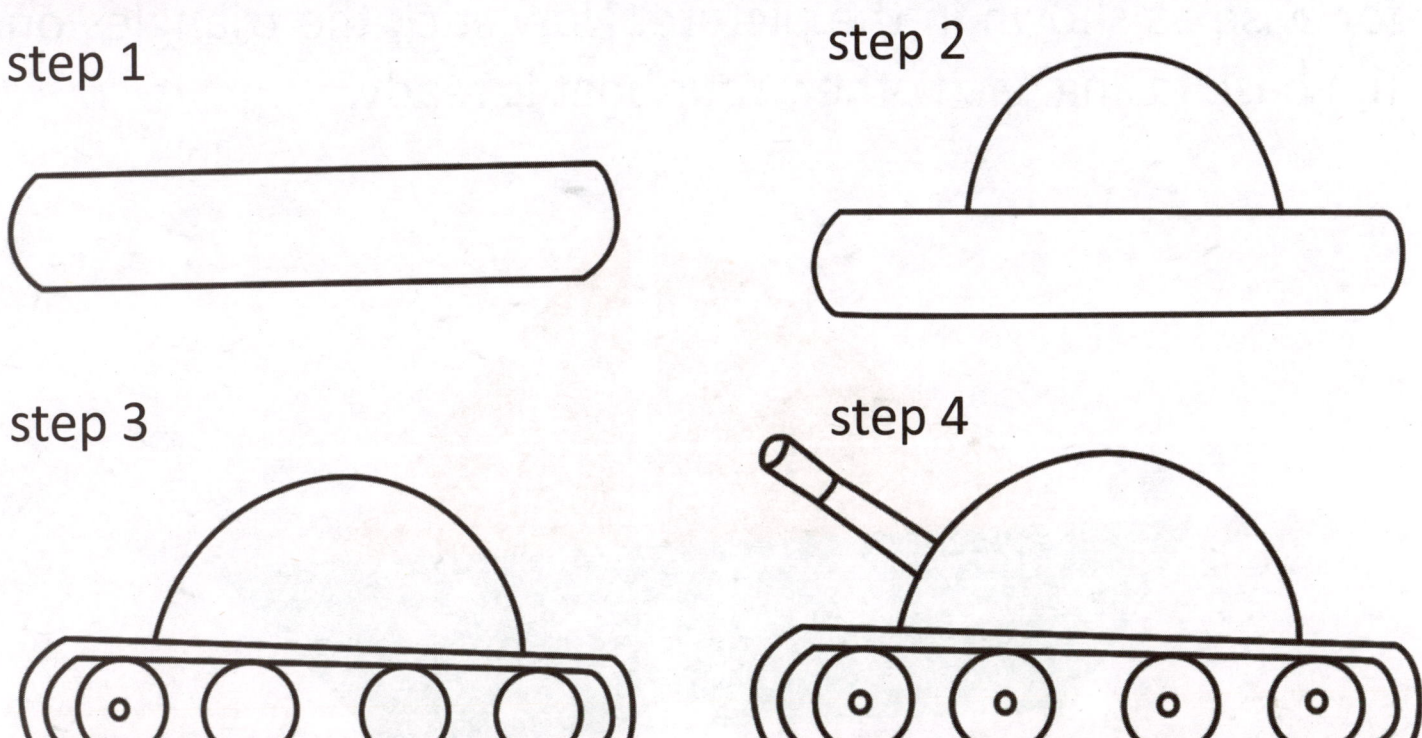

Make a paper boat following a few simple steps. Take glaze papers of two different colours. Cut one paper in two triangles and the other glaze paper for base as shown in the picture. Now stick the triangles on the base facing each other. Your boat is ready.

63 Help Billy catch the school bus.

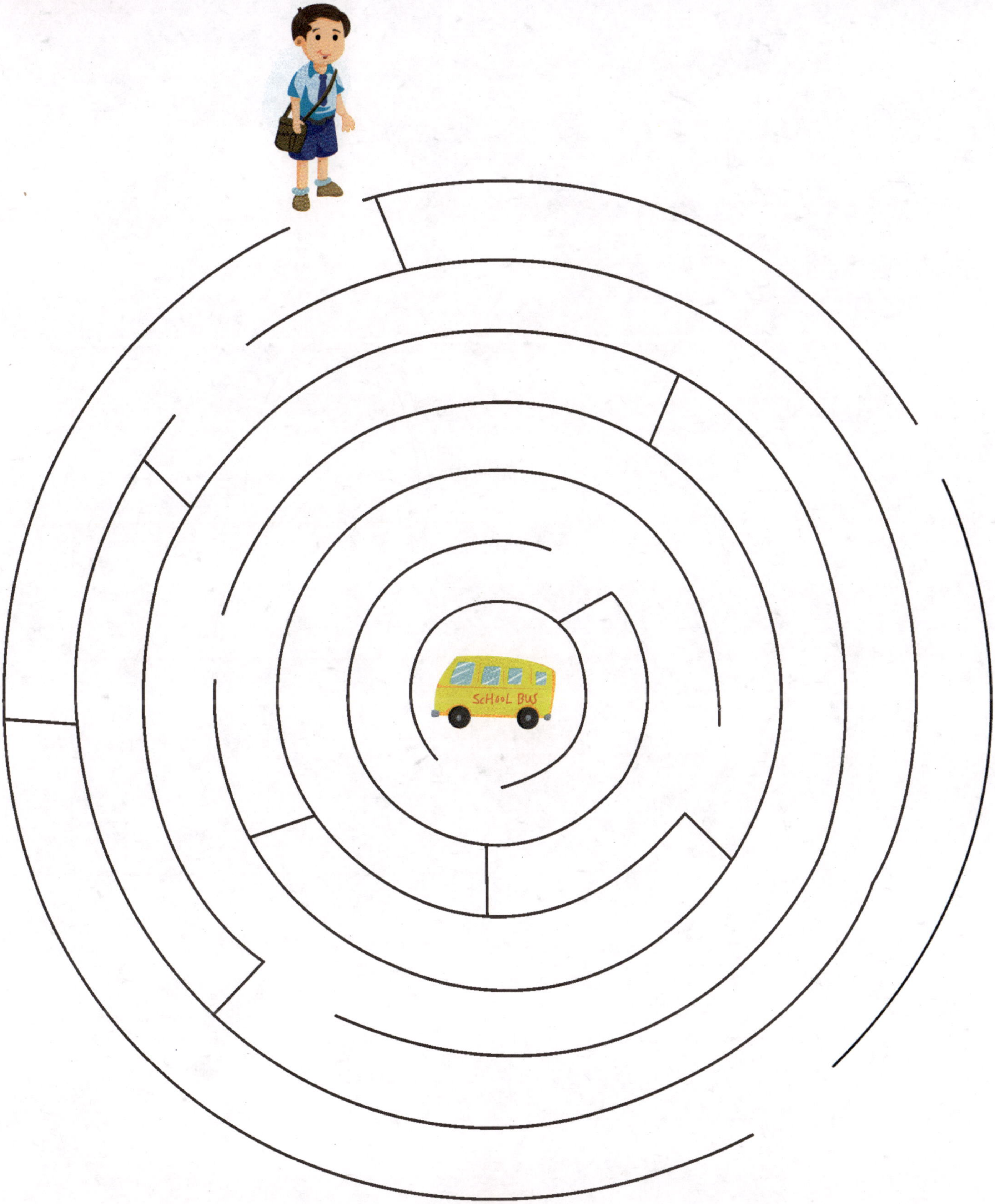

64 Join the dots and colour the car.

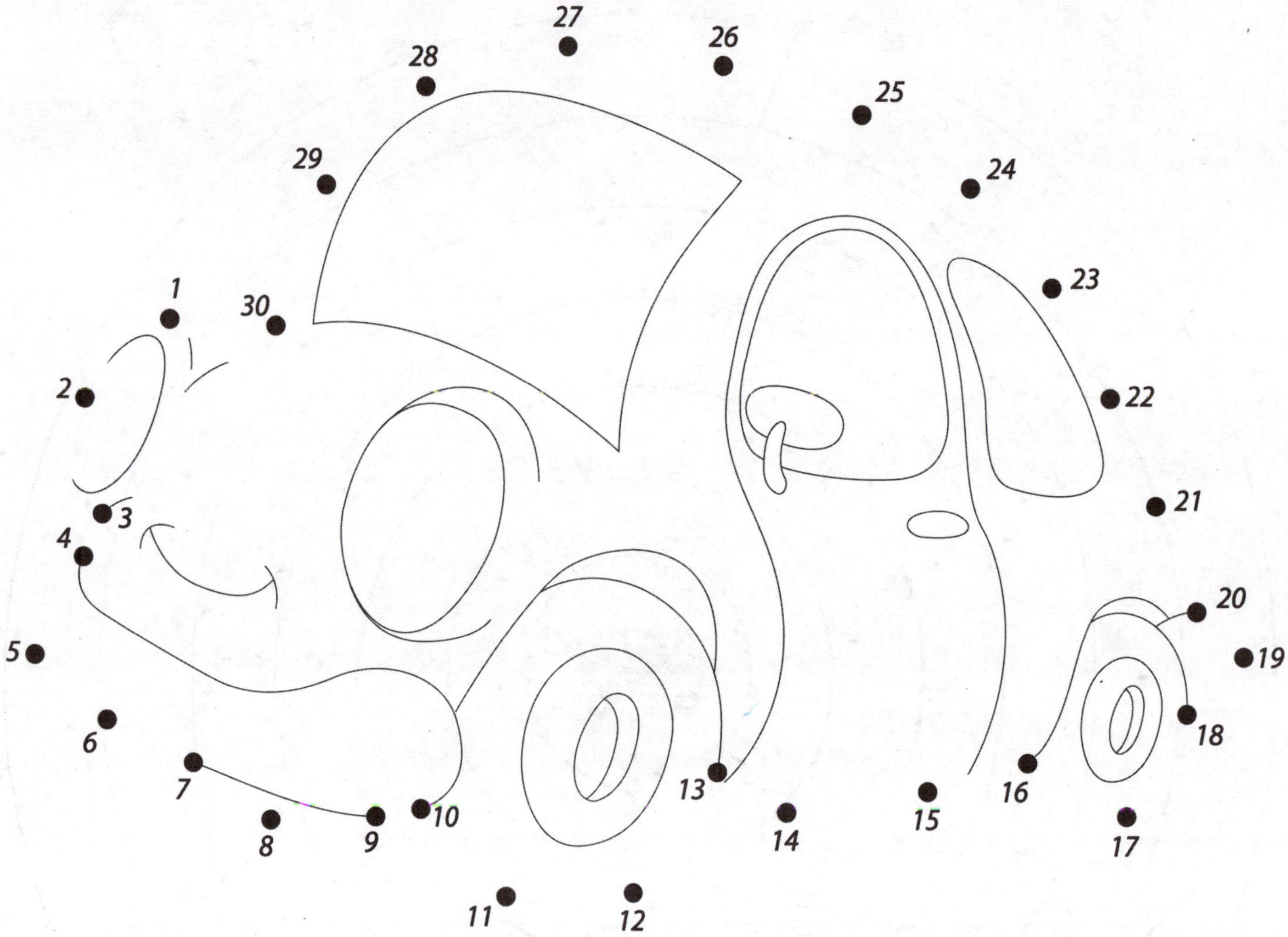

 Find out differences between the two.

66

Find out the below words in the word search grid and circle them.

Car / Truck / Bus / Bike / Train / Plane / Taxi / Subway / Van

Q	W	S	D	J	F	T	A	X	I
T	R	U	C	K	D	F	G	J	L
T	H	B	Z	X	A	L	X	P	Q
Y	Z	W	P	O	P	T	V	L	W
U	C	A	R	Y	X	R	C	A	E
I	L	Y	O	T	C	A	X	N	R
K	M	F	K	E	B	I	K	E	T
V	A	N	I	C	Z	N	B	U	S

67

Circle the odd one out in the below groups of pictures.

  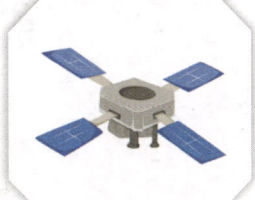  

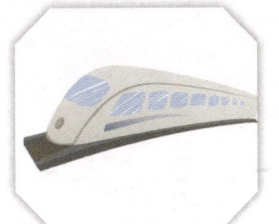    

68 Petrol is a fuel that is used in many means of transport. Tick the vehicles that run on petrol.

Colour the below picture of the ship.

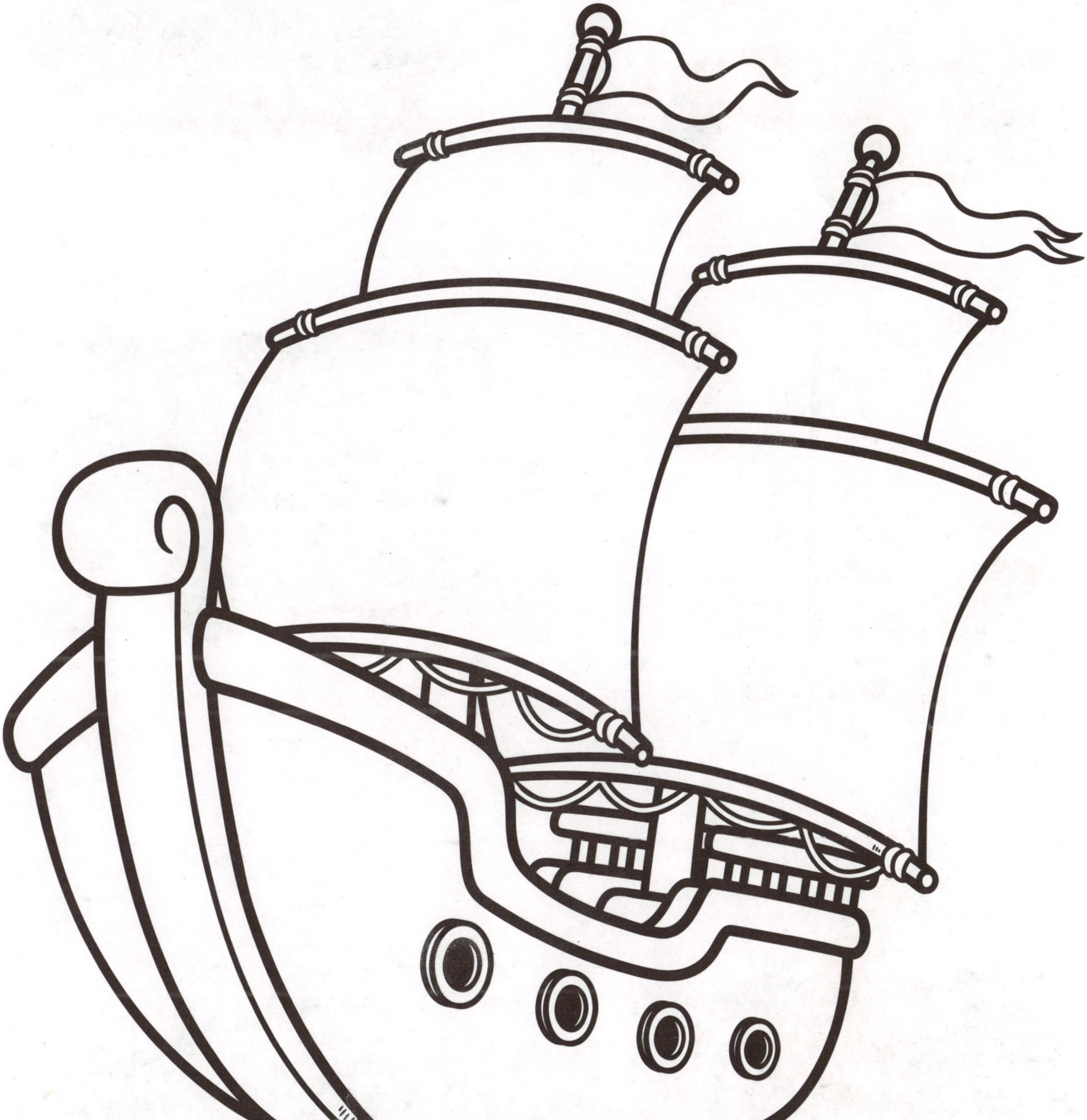

 Put a star against the vehicles that run on diesel.

71

Help the yellow car to get from point 1 to point 2.
Avoid the red circles.

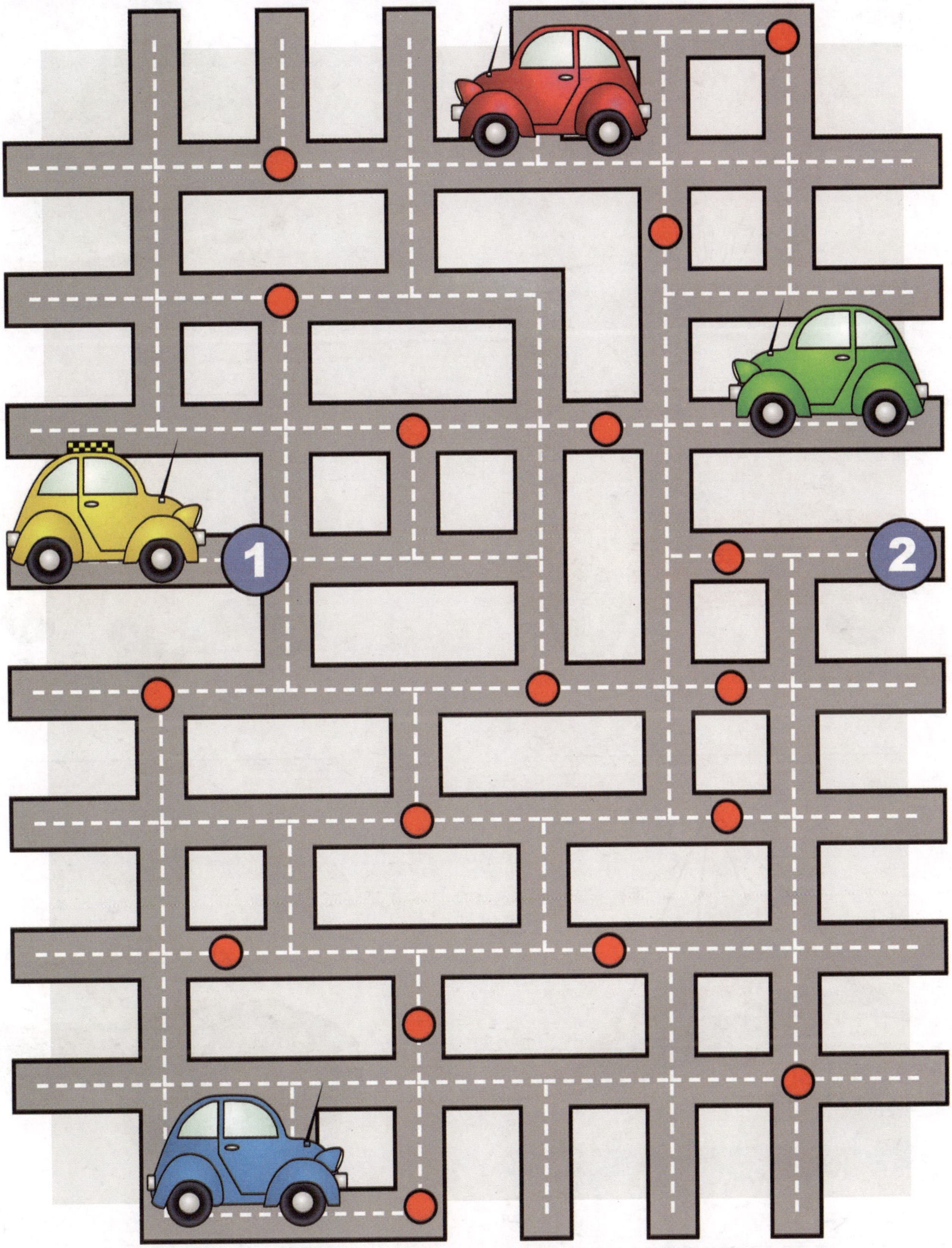

72 Write the names of below vehicles.

_____   _____

_____   _____

_____   _____

- Learn to make wooden raft.
- Take some wooden sticks and stick them adjacent to each other.//

- Now stick two sticks at one end and two sticks at the other end of the raft as shown in the picture below. Stick them firmly on the raft so that it doesn't move. Your raft is ready.

74 Colour the vehicles given below.

 Write the names of the vehicles given below.

_____   _____   _____

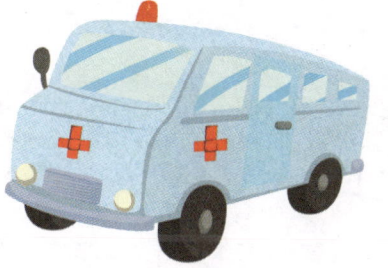  

_____   _____   _____

_____   _____   _____

76 Stick glaze paper of any colour and thermocol balls on the given outline of the ship.

Colour the means of transport as per the colour code mentioned below.

Road transport – Red

Air transport – Green

Water transport – Blue

78 Draw any vehicle of your choice and colour it.

79 John speaks about his routine. Complete the incomplete words.

John wakes up in the morning to go to school.

He takes the SCHOOL B_S to reach school and learns whole-heartedly.

John notices many LA_D TRA_SPORTS on the way like T_UCK, _AR, MO_ORCYCLE, BICY_LE, CRAN_, V_N and AMBULAN_E.

He passed by some R_IL transports as well as GOO_S TRAIN and FA_T TRAIN.

AIRPLA_E, PAR_CHUTE, H_T AIR BA_LOON were witnessed by John on his way back to home and he was very excited seeing these AI_ TRANSPORTS.

His excitement increased when one day, he saw something which he had never seen before from the bus window. It was a very big SHI_.

John returned home and told her mother what he saw. His mother told him that it was a WAT_R TRANSPORT.

Colour the car below. Now colour your thumb and press it on the window of the car.

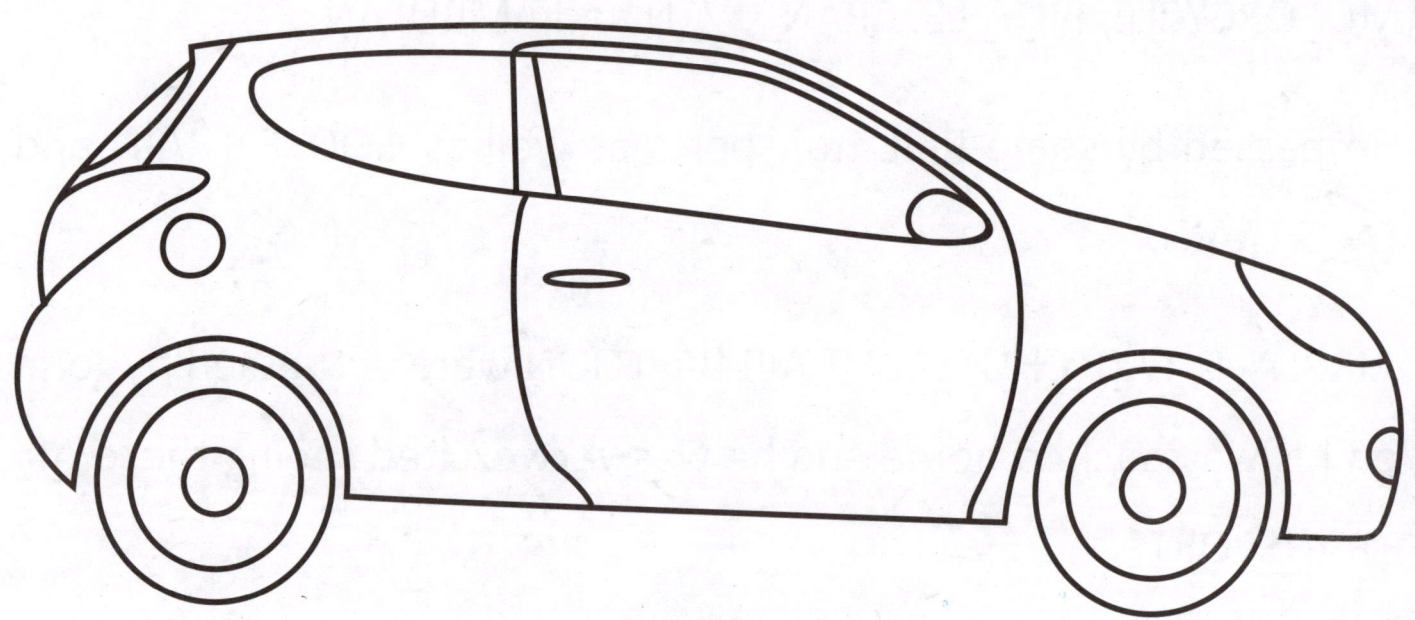

Circle the vintage vehicles below.

82 Join the dots to complete the helicopter.

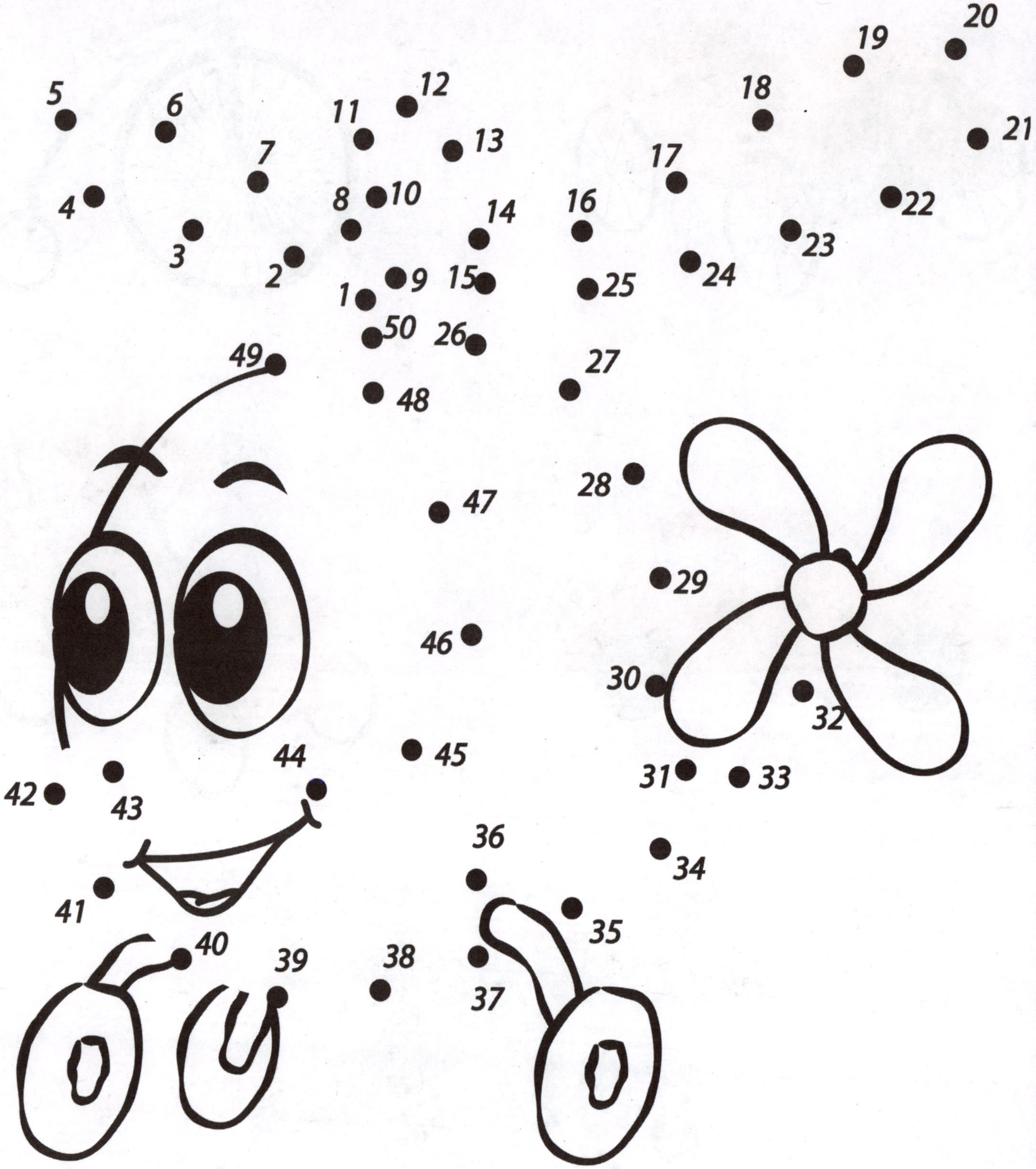

83 Help the car go through the maze and find petrol station.

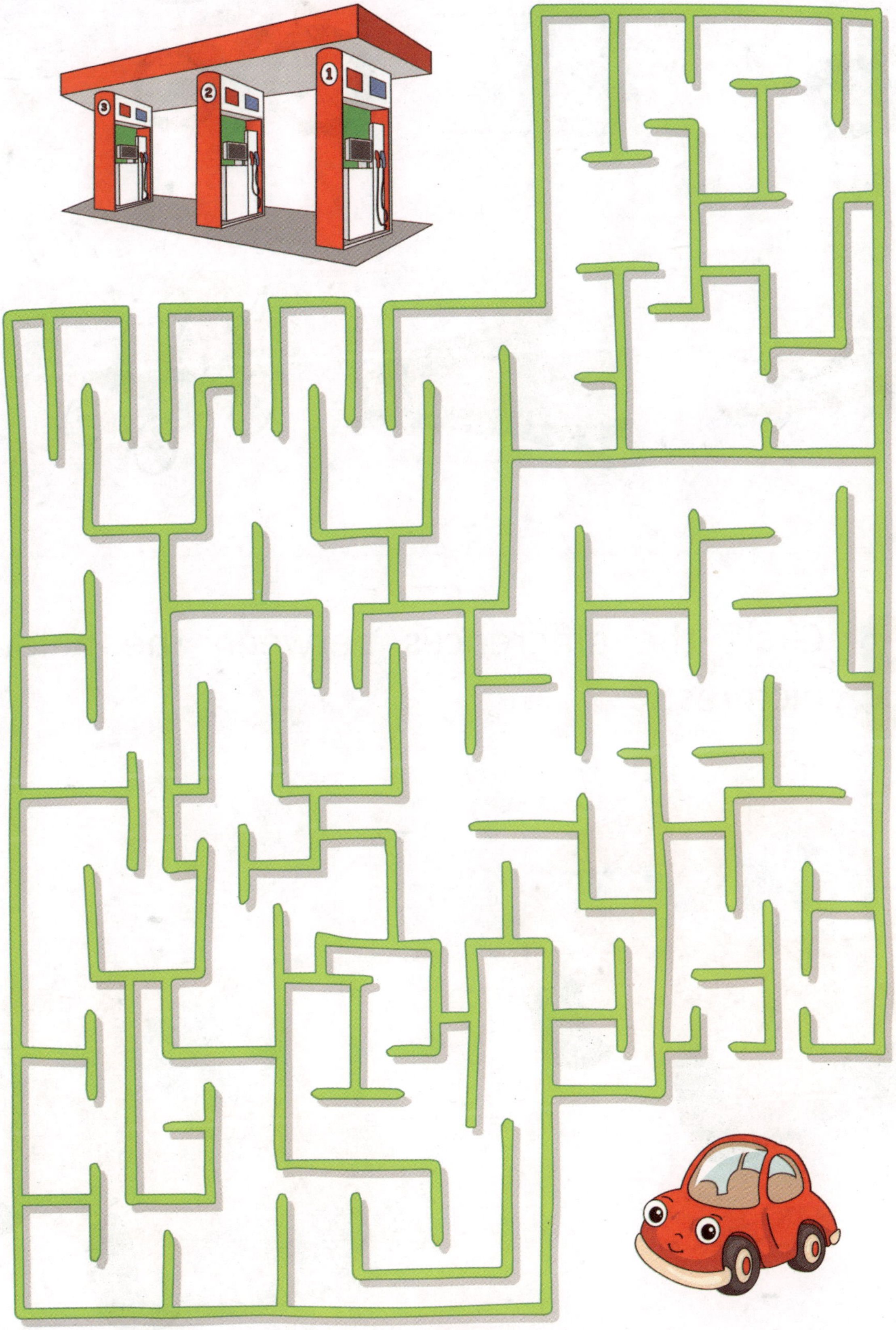

 Identify the mode of transport and write Air, Land, Water, Rail or Cable in the space provided.

 Circle the differences between the below two pictures.

86 Paste a picture of the modern means of transport whose ancient versions are given below.

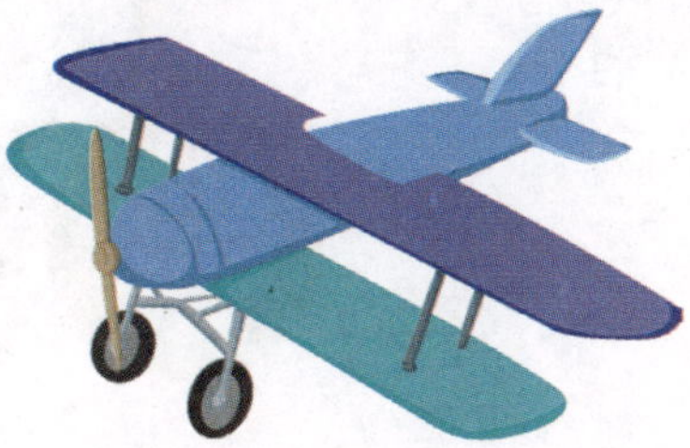

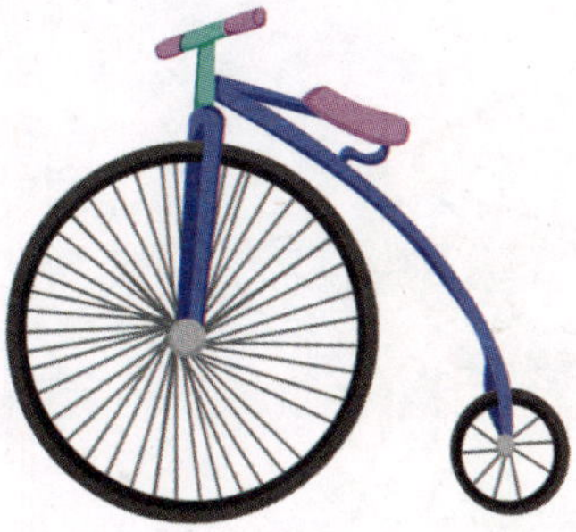

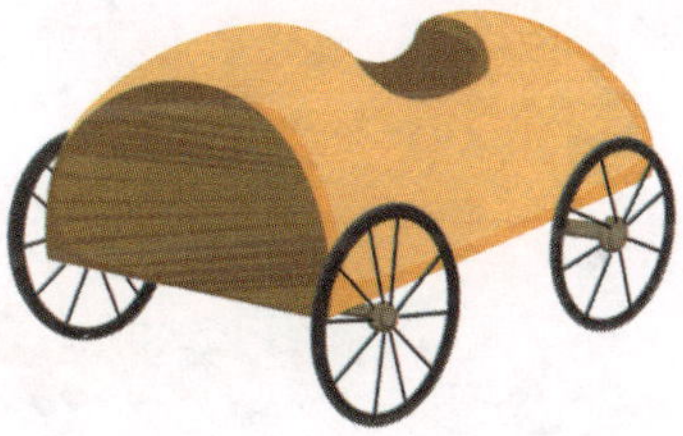

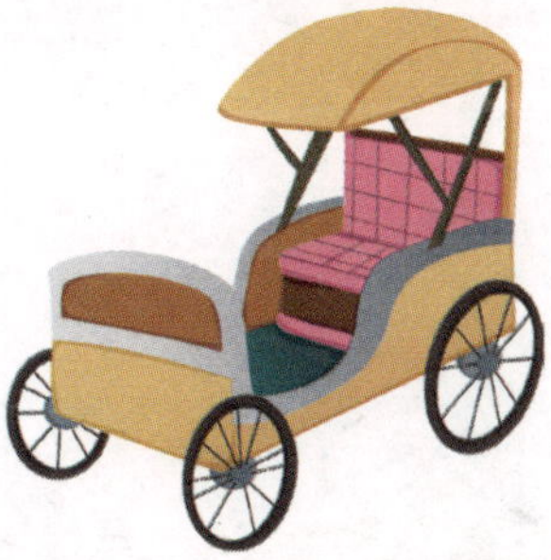

 You commute to different places shown below by different means. Match the places with their transport.

 Put a tick against 'Yes' if the statement is true and against 'No' if it's false.

All vehicles are four-wheeled	Yes ◯	No ◯
A unicycle has two wheels	Yes ◯	No ◯
A cable car transports people through cable	Yes ◯	No ◯
A truck transports goods	Yes ◯	No ◯
Train runs on rails	Yes ◯	No ◯
A ship transports oil, goods and people	Yes ◯	No ◯
Land transport flies in air	Yes ◯	No ◯

 Fill in the correct words from those given below.

Truck / Boat / Bike / Plane / Jet / Bus / Van / Cab / Train / Car

This vehicle has two wheels _____.

Another word for taxi is _____.

This vehicle has wings and starts with p _____.

This word rhymes with far _____.

This word rhymes with can _____.

A school _____ is big and yellow.

This word rhymes with float _____.

A garbage _____ picks up trash.

This word rhymes with get _____.

This vehicle travels on tracks _____.

90 Circle the correct words.

| Ambulance | Txai | Ipsh | Aireplan |

| Anbluance | Axit | Ship | Airplane |

| Anclubenca | Taxi | Spih | Apirane |

91 Join the below words to make a complete word.

Air + plane = _____

Row + boat = _____

Space + ship = _____

Motor + cycle = _____

Tug + boat = _____

Bi + cycle = _____

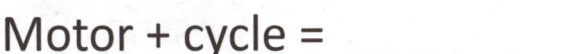

Try finding the following words in the word search grid given below.

T	A	N	K	F	V	J	K
A	I	R	P	L	A	N	E
X	W	Y	P	Z	N	Q	X
I	R	W	A	G	O	N	M
T	R	I	C	Y	C	L	E
T	R	A	C	T	O	R	N

Airplane

Taxi

Tractor

Tricycle

Tank

Van

Wagon

Fill in the blanks with correct words.

I fly on _____ to meet my grandfather in Oregon.

I ride my _____ to school.

My mother prefers to travel by _____.

My dad and I travelled the city by _____.

Kids are not allowed to ride a _____.

Some people use _____ to travel across the sea.

bicycle
car
motorcycle
ship
train
airplane

 The ship is about to halt at the stop. Navigate the captain to reach its destination.

 The clouds are missing in the below picture. Stick cotton to make clouds to depict that air transport is there in the sky.

 Satellites and spaceship are held up in space. Draw space to demonstrate the same. Colour the background black and add stars and a planet in the sky.

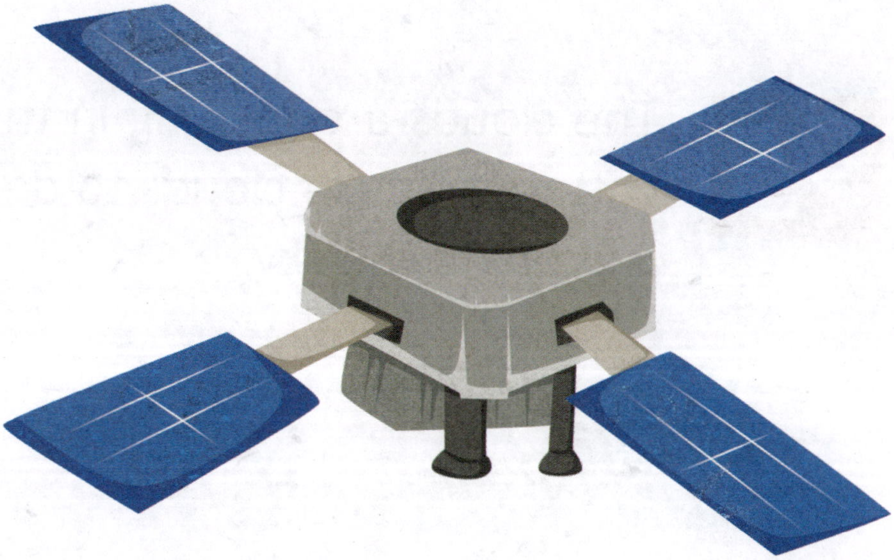

97 Match the correct options.

Students go to school in

Long distances are covered by

People like to travel over hills by

Two-wheeled vehicle is

Water transport is

98 Colour the transports with your favourite colours.

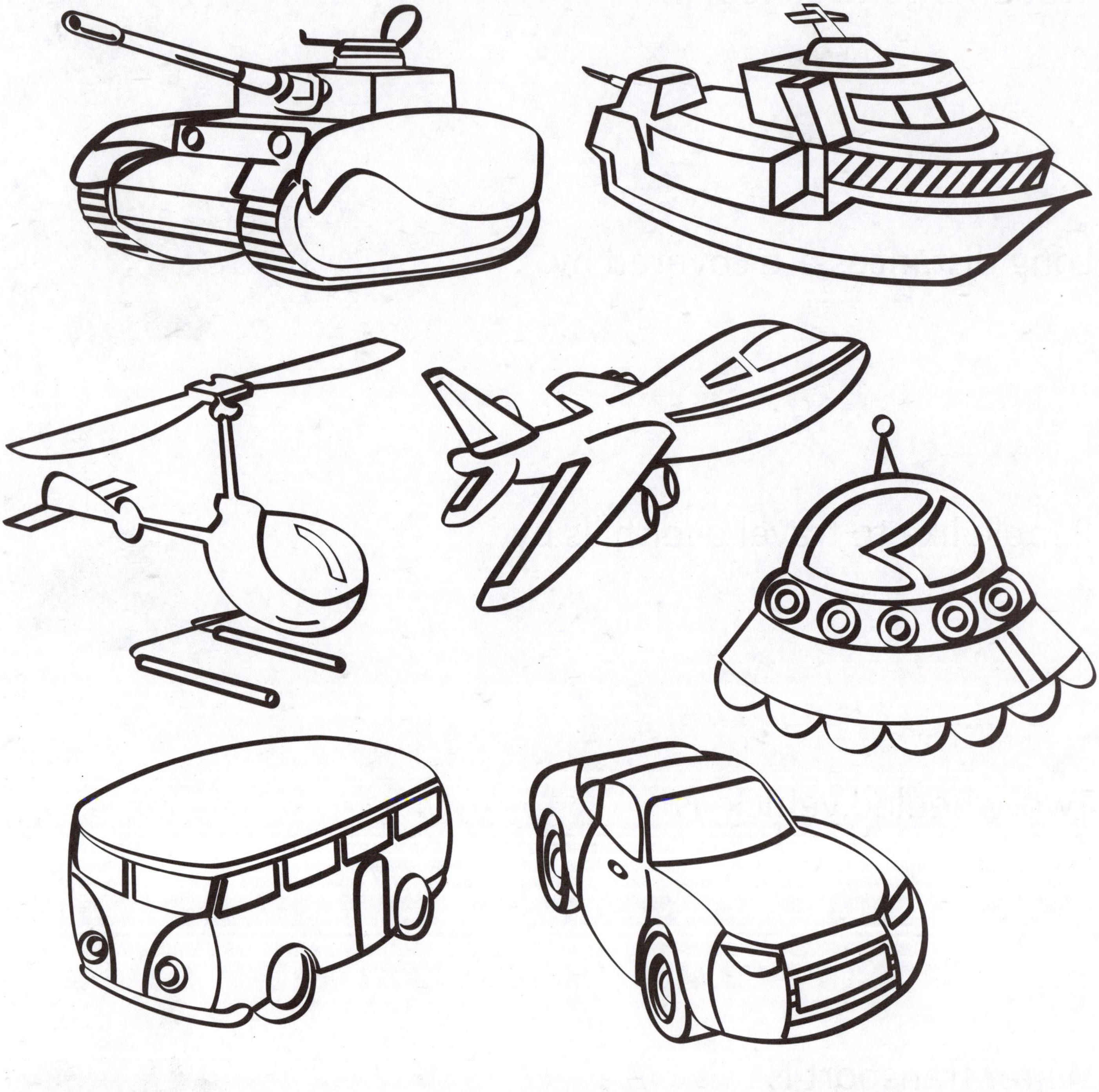

99 Make your favourite vehicle with molding clay.

100 Point out the differences between the two pictures given below.

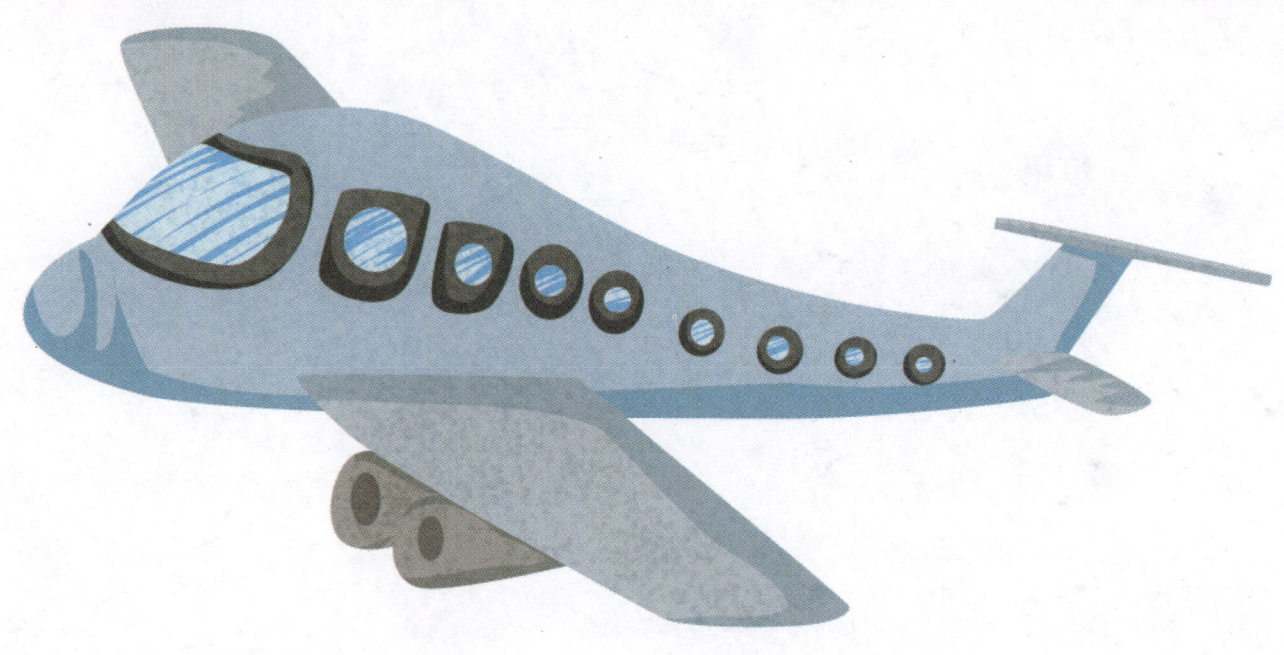

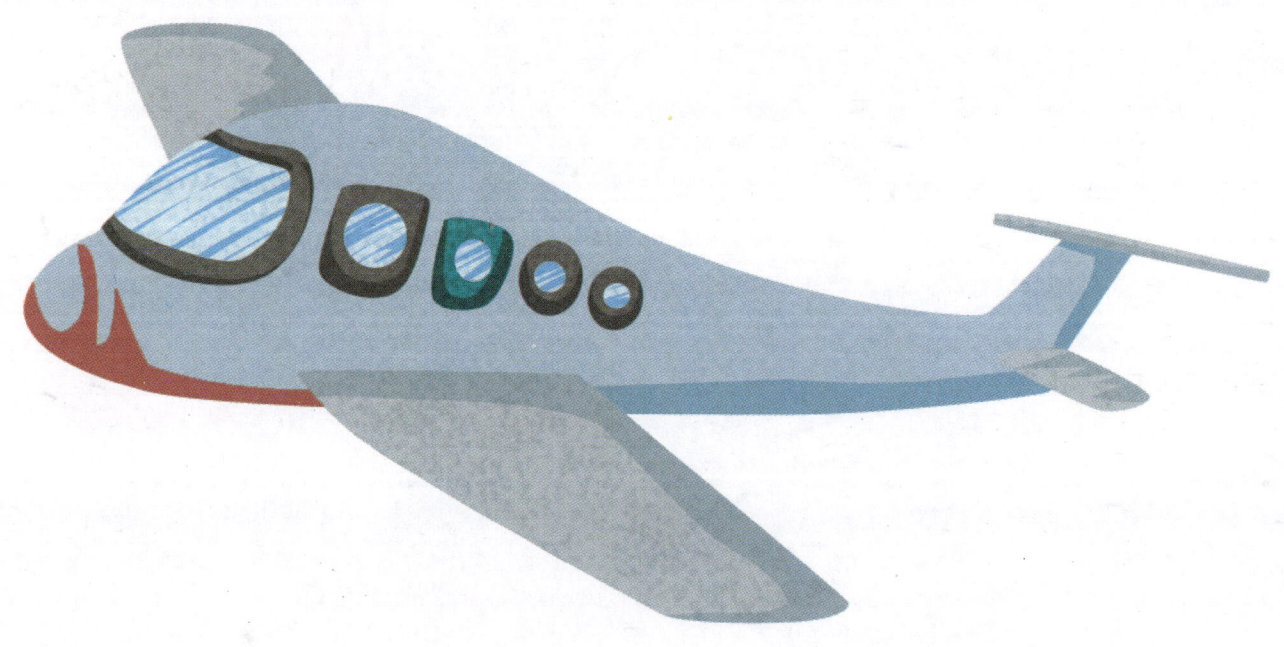